D0046563

# THE
# BURNING
# GROUND

# THE
# BURNING
# GROUND

Adam
O'Riordan

W. W. Norton & Company
*Independent Publishers Since 1923*
New York     London

For information about permission to reproduce selections
from this book, write to Permissions, W. W. Norton & Company, Inc.,
500 Fifth Avenue, New York, NY 10110

For information about special discounts for bulk
purchases, please contact W. W. Norton Special Sales at
specialsales@wwnorton.com or 800-233-4830

Manufacturing by Quad Graphics

Library of Congress Cataloging-in-Publication Data

Names: O'Riordan, Adam, 1982–, author.
Title: The burning ground / Adam O'Riordan.
Description: First American edition. | New York : W. W. Norton & Company,
[2017]
Identifiers: LCCN 2016059314 | ISBN 9780393239553 (hardcover)
Classification: LCC PR6065.R684 A6 2017 | DDC 823/.914—dc23
LC record available at https://lccn.loc.gov/2016059314

W. W. Norton & Company, Inc.
500 Fifth Avenue, New York, N.Y. 10110
www.wwnorton.com

W. W. Norton & Company Ltd.
15 Carlisle Street, London W1D 3BS

1 2 3 4 5 6 7 8 9 0

For Tom and Eva

For this is the real nature of California and the secret of its fascination; this untamed, undomesticated, aloof, prehistoric landscape which relentlessly reminds the traveller of his human condition and the circumstances of his tenure upon the earth. "You are perfectly welcome," it tells him, "during your short visit. Everything is at your disposal. Only, I must warn you, if things go wrong, don't blame me. I accept no responsibility. I am not part of your neurosis. Don't cry to me for safety. There is no home here. There is no security in your mansions or your fortresses, your family vaults or your banks or your double beds. Understand this fact, and you will be free. Accept it, and you will be happy."

—Christopher Isherwood

# Contents

# A Thunderstorm in Santa Monica

Harvey was sitting with Teresa in the courtyard of *Aguilo*, a fashionable restaurant on Abbott Kinney. They had come straight from the airport. Teresa would drop him at the house after lunch before returning to the office, but promised they would do something special that evening. This was Harvey's third trip to Los Angeles in the past eighteen months. He had met Teresa at a private view in London. She had been at Vassar with Eric Harkness, a friend who owned the advertising agency where he occasionally worked freelance as a copywriter. She was in the city looking to finance a film. At the private view she had mocked the untidy blocks of color on the massive canvases, each named after a Station of the Cross, and he had liked her for that. That night they had made love in her hotel suite overlooking Hyde Park. As Teresa slept, the sheets tangled around her legs, Harvey sat smoking in an armchair by the window, looking out at the chain of orange lamps winding through the deserted park.

At ten to six, after an hour dozing beside her, Harvey kissed Teresa on the ear and left. He heard her murmur as he clicked the door shut and had been surprised to find himself hesitating in the corridor, his corduroy jacket draped across his arm. The jacket smelled of fried food and damp, of his cramped studio apartment, with its three exterior walls and bad light after midday, where he had moved after his marriage had broken down.

A fortnight later her note arrived, alongside an envelope bearing his accountants' insignia and stamped URGENT. Eric must have given her the address. Teresa's letter asked him to come to Los Angeles. No strings, no promises. Why not? Harvey asked himself, as he rinsed a handful of cutlery in the sink, rubbing the cold tines of a fork with his thumb as he waited for the tap to run hot. It might be what he needed. Shake things up. Harvey borrowed the money for that first flight to LA from Eric, who watched from behind his desk, making a steeple of his stubby fingers as Harvey explained what the money was for. Harvey, in a tubular steel chair, tobacco tin on his knee, rolled a cigarette as he waited for Eric's response to his petition. "Go. Soak it in," Eric said in his terse, semi-Anglicized way as he tore the check from its book and slid it across the desk. He beckoned Harvey in for a hug—beaming, gregarious, like a small-town mayor, his arms spread wide before his chest. Harvey wondered if Eric and Teresa had once been lovers.

What had been a whim had now become an expensive and, Harvey knew, unsustainable habit. It wasn't the sex, the tide of Teresa's desire hard to navigate or predict; sometimes animalistic, his torso raised with welts and scratches as they lay together in the afterglow. Other times, as tentative as teenagers as Teresa's hands slowly mapped the geometry of Harvey's face. It wasn't the play at coupledom they made on strolls along Venice boardwalk past the street performers and panhandlers with their brassy handwritten signs. And it wasn't their in-jokes at the industry parties Teresa was obliged to attend, where they met and mocked with a look or squeeze of the hand the people, restless in their spheres, who came to court Teresa's influence. Otherworldly models teetering unsteady as foals in their high heels, their big, underwater eyes expressing a desire to act; downtrodden actors locked into five-year deals with prime-time shows, confessing a compulsion to direct; directors sick of being pushed around by studio heads, who now wanted to exec-produce for themselves. "I can confirm it: the earth is tipped toward Los Angeles, all the prettiest girls roll this way," Harvey told Eric one evening during that first trip, feeling alien and unfettered for the first time in years. He had Teresa pinned to an island table of a sports bar as he talked. They had retreated inside after walking by the ocean to see if they could catch a glimpse of the famous green flash said to appear on the horizon at sundown. "Here, Teresa wants to speak to you," Harvey said, passing the phone, looking up at the massive glistening athletes, sweat-drenched on the big screens around the bar.

No, it wasn't any of these things, Harvey told himself. What he was hooked on, he was sure, was the eleven-hour lacuna of the flight and all it entailed. It began at takeoff. The cabin hushed. The cutlery rattling in the galley as the plane gained speed, the plastic cabin beginning to creak. The engines roaring like beasts heard from the bowels of an amphitheater. The focused quiet of an examination hall as passengers concentrated on keeping calm and pretending what was happening was perfectly normal. The plane would continue to ascend, the patchwork of fields dropping away below as London's suburbs petered out into countryside. As the plane gained height Harvey would feel his body respond, increasing the pressure on his heels, righting itself as it tried to adjust to the altitude. Until the nose of the plane dropped a few degrees and the plangent note of the electronic gong told passengers takeoff was over and they were free to undo their seat belts. After the thrill of takeoff came the endurance test of the hours midair. He would start and then abandon films, leaving their protagonists frozen on the small screen. Harvey relished this restlessness, the boredom of a quality last known in childhood. Then would come a few hours of fitful sleep. Slack-mouthed, snapping awake as his neck gave under the weight of his head.

Then, just when the tedium seemed interminable, the limbo of the flight never ending, the captain would come over the intercom and announce the final hour in the air and the beginning of the descent. Then came the prospect of landing and the dissipating tension as time reengaged and found its thrust. Now the plane would pass for miles over Los Angeles, the low-rise city; its dense acreage of parking lots and freeways punctuated by the oasis of a baseball ground or a football field; the light charged with a biblical intensity. Looking out to the brown mountains that hemmed in the city and seemed to drive its seething mass toward the ocean. Then the sound of the landing gear like a winch hauling the world below toward the belly of the plane and a final thrill: that burst of speed toward the runway. Then the judder as the plane touched down, past the tower and the terminals until he could make out the faces of the baggage handlers and engineers in their coveralls. Then the spell was broken. He would adjust his watch. He was certain it was this—not Teresa, not the distance from his life in London—that he had come to crave.

In the courtyard of *Aguilo*, a bank of railway sleepers and an ivy-covered wall provided shade from the swimming-pool-size section of sky. Teresa was busy at her BlackBerry straining to hear over the noise of the lunchtime crowd, as she pushed the glossy black tear of the headset into her ear. She looked over to Harvey who had paused his meal, anxious not to finish before Teresa had started hers. She flashed two fingers at him, grimacing theatrically. Harvey set down his fork and watched a Mexican busboy in his fifties deliver a baked egg floating in a pool of green lentils to a pregnant woman at the table opposite. A skinny compatriot refilled her water glass. A blond waiter with a clover tattooed behind his ear hovered nearby with his notepad, as if scoring their performance.

Harvey inspected himself in the back of his spoon. His eyes were puffy from the flight. He was still a little tanned from his last trip out. The lines on his brow had grown deeper over the past few years. He tilted the spoon to inspect the few silver strands that had recently appeared at his temples. As Teresa continued her conversation Harvey noticed a girl in a floral-print dress, looking up at him from her dessert. She could be no more than nineteen, wore no makeup or had been made up to appear as if she wasn't wearing any. Harvey couldn't decide. She had a soft, cherubic face and wore two slides in her short hair in an attempt to suppress the natural curl or disguise a recent change in length. He caught her eye and she looked away.

Harvey glanced over to Teresa, still on the phone, the food on her plate untouched. She had been there to meet him at the airport. He had spotted her checking her watch by the Arrivals board. Teresa would be forty-eight next month. Compared to the girl she had an unshowy beauty, but she carried herself with a lightness that was itself girlish. When Teresa had spotted Harvey at Arrivals, she had run to hug him. She had brought him flowers: huge sunflowers, their long stems wrapped in brown paper. Harvey imagined her picking them out, double-parked outside the florist on Washington Boulevard, shaking her head at the alternatives before holding out a crisp twenty when the right bunch was proffered. All this without breaking from her conversation on her BlackBerry.

"You made it!" Teresa had said. Then pulling him close into her, "So good to have you back, baby."

The plane had been empty when Harvey boarded. At check-in he had gambled on a seat in a central section between the bulkheads. In front of his seat there was a fold-down platform for a bassinet. Harvey had reasoned that a midweek midday flight to Los Angeles would not be full of families. As a tinny aria was pumped through the cabin, he wondered if he might have the whole row to himself. He changed into his complimentary flight socks, pushed his shoes out of sight below his seat and buckled himself in. Contemplating the flight ahead he closed his eyes.

"Nick Antonopoulos," said a voice.

The words pulled him from a maze of memories, a fervid series of unconnected images, summoned before takeoff in his semidreaming doze. The voice repeated:

"Nick Antonopoulos."

Harvey opened his eyes this time and looked at the hand held out to him. Standing above him was a man in his thirties. He was dressed in khaki slacks, the crease ironed sharp down the front of each leg, and a black long-sleeved polo shirt, the shining nylon like something a professional golfer might wear. His dark hair was clipped militarily short around his ears and at his neck. He seemed generically clean-cut, politely forthright, indistinguishable from many other Americans you might meet in airport lounges traveling on business across the western world. He was smiling softly, a large and sensual mouth, a smile that suggested he was amused by the archetype he found himself inhabiting. Nick Antonopoulos gave off the impression that the two men shared a long-standing arrangement to meet and that he was now finally making himself known. Harvey offered his own hand and attempted to stand, before realizing this was impractical.

"Second flight of the day for me," Nick said, smiling more broadly now as he unpacked his briefcase.

He pulled out a magazine. On the cover were arrayed pyramids of unnaturally bright apples and oranges. As he sat down Nick gestured to the cover and explained that he worked in the fruit industry. He had spent the previous night in Versailles, in what he described as a *heinously* small hotel room, where he had been attending his firm's annual European sales conference. He was now flying to Los Angeles, deputizing for his manager at the International Conference where he would be delivering a paper on the drivers and barriers behind consumers' fresh fruit choices. He would be flying back to England after two nights at the Four Seasons on Doheny. At first the men exchanged a few platitudes: the clichés and curiosities of international travel; stories from Nick's life on the road, told with great exuberance where little actually happened. A mention of his wife and two daughters at home in Windsor where they had moved recently, and where, walking through the Great Park one day with his daughter, he was sure he had seen Queen Elizabeth drive past.

As the plane taxied toward the foot of the runway, Nick took a mobile phone from his briefcase. He scrolled through the names, then pressed his thumb on the touchpad.

"Samantha?"

Something in the sureness of Nick's responses gave Harvey an unexpected comfort.

"OK. About to take off now. Love to the kids. Talk later. I know. I know," and then with a lingering smile, "OK."

Nick finished his call and turned off the phone, gesturing with a raised palm to the air-hostess who had been approaching with a frown. He turned and flashed a smile at Harvey.

When they hit the turbulence Harvey was sleeping. The map on the headrest screen was the first thing he saw when he opened his eyes. They were somewhere over northern Canada. The jolt was so hard it lifted him from his seat, his lap belt biting into the top of his pelvis. He glanced to his right and saw Nick gripping his armrests, bracing himself against the movements of the plane. The plane was rattling harder now, throwing passengers from side to side. Harvey heard a sharp intake of breath from an air-hostess as she pulled herself along the aisle to the jump seat. He watched as she exchanged a brief and unmistakably fearful glance with her colleague in the aisle opposite. Now the noise of the engines increased as if struggling to keep the plane airborne. Harvey knew something was terribly wrong. An elderly woman in the row to their right had begun to sob and was being comforted by her husband, who was patting her bony shoulder ineffectually with one hand, while gripping his armrest with the other. Her husband's single-serving wine bottle had fallen from his tray and was cannoning along the aisle as the plane was buffeted roughly. Harvey thought of the footage he had once seen of an office during an earthquake in the Philippines. Then he thought about the flight deck, as he knew from the reconstructions he had watched on TV, the pilots wrestling at their dual controls trying desperately to keep the plane aloft, some series of fatal mistakes already placing them beyond safety. Harvey was sure this was the end. In a moment the plane would be lost in vast white tracts below. It would be days before the rescue parties reached them, or what parts of them were left. Their luggage, the bright clothes picked out for beach holidays in California, would be strewn for miles across the snow. It was then that Nick placed his hand on top of Harvey's. He gripped it strongly with a force that left Harvey in no doubt it was deliberate, before returning it to his own armrest. Neither man looked at the other but it was understood by Harvey that he had been reached out to in his last moments. That humanity had prevailed and that men had faced their fate together. They endured several minutes more of extreme turbulence before the plane's movements became at first less frequent and then less severe. The first officer came over the intercom to announce they had hit several big pockets of air as they passed around a storm front and that as they were expecting a little more chop up ahead, he would be leaving the seat-belt sign on for now. The first officer sounded relieved to be delivering this news.

As the flight wore on, both men retreated into themselves but Nick continued to offer the same amused, ironic smile whenever Harvey got up to stretch his legs or use the toilet. Harvey watched Nick scrolling through spreadsheets on a laptop, biting the thumbnail on one hand while running the forefinger of the other down the columns of numbers. As they waited to disembark, standing in the aisle of the business class section, the empty seats littered with newspapers and magazines, Nick turned to Harvey and offered him his card. "This is me. Keep in touch," he smiled, and patted Harvey on the back. Harvey placed the card in his pocket. He wanted to thank Nick Antonopoulos, if not for his company—for a few minutes of conversation over the eleven hours in the air could hardly be called company—then for his proximity. To tell him of the unexpected comfort his fleeting companionship had given him. He felt he was taking leave of an old friend. But instead he nodded and smiled and said, "Yes, thanks, well, good luck with everything."

Harvey stood in the empty living room of Teresa's house, more drunk than he would have expected to

be from the bottle of Gavi at *Aguilo*. When Teresa
had dropped him off she had pointed out an elderly
neighbor in front of one of the smaller houses across
the street, staring at them from below a Stars and
Stripes the size of a double bedspread that flew above
his lawn. "Poor Republicans. Worst kind," Teresa said
as Harvey got out of the car. "I'll see you later." She
had waved an arm from the window as she drove off.
The house was between owners—Teresa had taken
up a series of sublets since selling her own place in
the Palisades. She was waiting for the market to even
out before buying somewhere new, probably farther
up the coast toward Malibu. Where, in her fantasy
life, she would hike and paddleboard every weekend
and buy two Weimaraners and walk the ghost-gray
gundogs out along the shining sands each evening.
But as she had to travel so often for work this place was
fine for now. The living room of Teresa's house was
bare except for a few sticks of furniture: an oversize
easy chair that sat on top of two thick wooden rock-
ers, some wilted roses in a narrow-necked vase, a pair
of shot-silk curtains in translucent green that only
partially covered the doors leading onto the brick
terrace with its hip-height wall and the small lawn
slanting upward above it. Harvey walked through
the rooms of the house, absentmindedly opening
and closing the closets and drawers. This was the
third rental Harvey had visited Teresa in. No matter

how earnestly she talked about the life she planned in Malibu, she seemed drawn to these temporary, transitory, anonymous spaces, the residue of someone else's life hanging about them still.

He walked into the bedroom and stood under a lacquered wooden fan on to which four flower-shaped light-fittings were fixed. As he looked at the made-up bed Harvey remembered his last trip. The afternoon he arrived Teresa had been lying reading a script with the cover across her as Harvey dressed after showering. She had drawn back the duvet to reveal her naked lower half, instructing him to "kiss it." She had smelled of fresh laundry and as he kissed her, as asked, he had tasted that unmistakable sweet, dry alkaline. He sat for a moment on the corner of the bed looking at a pile of jewelry on Teresa's bedside table, the rings and fine chain-link bracelets tangled up inside on another, remembering that summer afternoon when the tang of eucalyptus came through the open window.

The crows were loud in the garden outside, their raw cawing and flapping audible. Harvey went into the en suite bathroom. The surfaces were crammed with conditioners and beauty creams with French names: Beurre de Karité and Crème Vital. Harvey took a towel from the bar and, walking back through the bedroom and out of the sliding doors, arranged it for sunbathing on the lawn. He lay back and felt his face warming in the sun. He closed his eyes and tried to reconstruct the face of the girl from *Aguilo*. He tried to imagine what she might look like naked. Her high breasts, the silvery down in the small of her back, her long, tan, slightly bowed legs. How her skin might smell up close in the well of her collarbone or might feel as he ran his fingertips across it. If she would taste like Teresa or if she would have some different tang or musk. Unthinking, he tucked his erection under the belt of his jeans, rolled over on to his front and took a cigarette from the box. There was a single match left hanging from the book he had picked up at a bar back in London. He bent the head back against the strike-strip and clicked his fingers. He lit the cigarette and let the burning match fall onto the grass. He took a long drag, then watched the blue ribbons of smoke from his cigarette dissolve into the clear sky. Above him he heard a single-propeller plane heading toward Catalina. He looked up at the acacia in the far corner of the garden, the fringe of late afternoon light around its outer edge. He thought back to the last view of London from the cab on the way to the airport. How the trees were nearly bare. He remembered the wet leaves on the pavements and the gardens of the Victorian houses as he waited in traffic.

As the afternoon wore on Harvey worked his way through a pile of old magazines, Italian and French

*Vogues*, that Teresa had stacked in the corner of the living room. Picking up a new magazine every time he went inside to light another cigarette from the stove the previous owner had painstakingly restored, that Teresa had told him about in the car on the way over, the makers' names, O'Keefe and Merritt, how the previous owner couldn't afford to have it shipped to his new place. Harvey's cigarette butts littered the terrace like the droppings of a caged bird. He thought he should collect them before Teresa got back, which would be any time now. As he lay out in the garden, the light softening, the late sun sluicing over his closed eyes, he felt a heaviness fall over him. He told himself he must not sleep.

He was woken a few moments later by the telephone. By the time he reached it the answer-machine had kicked in. He listened to Teresa's voice:

"Harvey, baby, I have some bad news." There was a pause. "I have to fly to New York . . . tonight. Don't be mad," then as if angered by her display of weakness, "I told you when you booked your ticket this was always a possibility."

Then she added in a staccato burst, "The car's at the studio. Won't be more than a couple of days. I'll call you from the airport."

Harvey thought he should be angry but registered that anger was not forthcoming. He walked out into the garden and stood on the brick terrace. The light was fading now and a sliver of crescent moon was clear in the blue sky. Teresa's neighbors were home. He had heard their car pull up as he listened to her message. Now he was back in the garden and heard them bickering behind the flannel bush separating the two properties. Then their back door slamming, followed by the sound of a man pedaling hard on an exercise bike in the garden. Harvey's drowsiness had lifted. Maybe some exercise would do him good. He would take a stroll. Closing the doors to the garden, he pulled a woolen sweater from his hand luggage and picked up the spare set of keys from the counter.

It was a short walk from the house to Lincoln Boulevard, where the freshly mown lawns suddenly gave on to four lanes of loud traffic and neon signs. Harvey walked along Lincoln past the strip malls offering manicures and discount household goods, the ten-dollar tire balancing, the car lots and charity shops with rotating signs on their roofs, past the taco shack where he had eaten hog maws with Teresa on his first trip out. The only other pedestrians were off to work night shifts or, having served their purpose for the day, were waiting at the bus stops to be ferried out of the city. Harvey had ridden on one on his first visit when Teresa had been delayed and unable to meet him at the airport. It had seemed to him a kind of mobile psychiatric ward, where the ill and the underpaid were condemned to spend their days. He stopped a few blocks before Pico outside a bar that advertised itself as a "British Pub and Restaurant." The exterior was painted to resemble the whitewashed wattle-and-daub of an English country cottage. He peered in through the tinted and unwashed windows. The bar was hung with photographs of soccer players from the 1970s, some of whom he recognized, and faded reproduction advertisements for ale. He decided to go in. He took a seat at the bar and ordered a glass of lager, looking up at the three antique horse brasses set in the ceiling beams, a collection someone had begun and then clearly abandoned.

The barmaid who served him had looked younger in the gloom as he had entered the bar, but up close Harvey saw the skin on her face was heavily lined and creased from what could only be decades of overexposure to the sun. She set the drink down on a paper napkin in front of him, strings of bubbles rising up inside the amber glass. "What's that?" a grizzled man with a muzzle of pure white stubble, wearing a foam baseball cap with the name of a local moving company on it, called out to the barmaid as she flicked through the channels on the TV above the bar. "Storm. Blowing in from Alaska. Time to go home, old man," she said, patting his arm. Harvey waved his glass at the barmaid, who promptly set another beer down in front of him. Perched on his stool, Harvey watched the bar fill up. The after-work crowd of middle managers and studio assistants, here to shoot a few frames of pool or watch a soccer game on the big screen. Harvey watched a pockmarked, mustachioed man flirting with a fat Latina. It seemed almost everyone in the bar was talking about the storm, questioning the barmaid, who was now the self-appointed authority on the subject, as they came to order more drinks. There was an atmosphere of growing excitement and anticipation in the crowded room as if a foreign dignitary were visiting the city. The bar filled up and then thinned out again but Harvey kept to his stool drinking steadily, unnoticed among the regulars. Before he left he changed three dollar bills into quarters. The barmaid was reluctant to spare the change until Harvey waved a thumb in the direction of the pool table in its tent of fluorescent light. Looking at his watch, in the second it took the numbers to swim into focus, Harvey saw that it was getting on for midnight now and he was drunk. He staggered on to Pico, the electric power lines on their wooden poles buzzing above him. He wanted to see the Pacific Ocean, to be near that massive expanse of water. To hear the waves breaking on the sand of Santa Monica State Beach, the fierce hiss as each one sank into the shore.

It was raining as the pier came into view but Harvey could make out the lights of the fairground that occupied part of it. As if the big wheel was reeling in the weather from out at sea. Mountainous inky clouds formed on the horizon. His sweater was soaking, the wet wool releasing an acrid, peroxide smell. As he scrambled up the terrace of plantings to the mouth of the pier, Harvey spotted a phone booth and stumbled toward it. He fed a handful of quarters into the slot and punched in a number. The phone rang several times before someone picked up.

"Nick, Nicky?"

The person on the other end of the line swallowed. Harvey heard the whistle and sigh of heavy nasal breathing, then the sound of someone rolling over heavily and faintly behind that the springs of the mattress.

"Nick, it's Harvey . . . from the plane."

"Mmmm." Then nothing but the crackle of the line.

"I wondered if . . . if you wanted to meet? For a drink or something?"

"Mmmm," lower this time. There was a pause and a soft click, then a recorded voice instructed Harvey to replace the receiver.

The rain was falling heavily now, bouncing high off the slats of the pier, blurring the lights of the houses farther up the coast. Harvey stepped over the guardrail and made his way down the deserted pier as if walking out onto a frozen lake, the boards slippery under his feet. The lights of the fairground rides were reflected in the pooling water. He looked out to the ocean as the first fork of lightning split the sky. He imagined Nick Antonopoulos rolling back to sleep, waking early to call his wife and run through his speech for the sales conference. Wondering what had disturbed him in the night, the memory of someone using his name and wondering if he had dreamed it. Teresa, midair, working through a list of red-flagged emails. He thought of the storm clouds forming earlier in the day over the Gulf of Alaska, the pressure driving them down the length of the country, over Point Conception with its white lighthouse where they had picnicked last trip, all the way down to Santa Monica, the rain taking shape then falling on the lanes of traffic on Lincoln Boulevard. He stood at the end of the pier at what seemed like the very tip of this city. He listened to the thunder out at sea. A white line of lightning cut sideways through the cloud bank. He would stay here a while longer, Harvey thought, and see the storm through.

# The El Segundo Blue Butterfly

I

I am fourteen years old, on the backseat of a bus heading downtown. The seat covers are blue and faded, tiny lines of jade woven through the fabric. I'm watching dust motes spiral through diagonals of sunlight. The worn floor is sticky, and it glitters where the light is hitting it. In a copy of yesterday's *Daily News*, abandoned on the seat next to me, I read that the El Segundo Blue Butterfly is now officially endangered. Last term I was chosen from a staff of twenty at the school newspaper, the *Sentinel*, to interview Michael Hogan Bernstein, the financier to whom Channel 7 recently dedicated a half-hour special. I am on my way to meet him at his office in the City National Tower. The air conditioner has broken down. I can smell diesel and feel the engine through my seat. Someone called Amancio has scratched their name onto the window. I look down onto the shining roofs of the cars on the freeway. We pass a sign for the Prophecy Speaks Bible Lectures and the Blue Oyster Cult at the Pavilion.

My mother was up late with me last night going over my questions. I have them written on a sheet of notepaper from a set that was a gift from a customer at the laundry two Christmases ago. My mother had taken the afternoon off to help me prepare. Her section at the front of Triple-A on Coolridge Avenue sitting empty. I imagine it without her: the neon alterations sign in the window, the sewing machine on the Dresden-lace cloth that belonged to her grandmother, the fine cones of colored thread on the wooden rack on the wall, the dresses and suits hung in their plastic sheaths waiting for her to mend them. It is only the second day she has taken off since my father left when I was seven years old.

She stands in her housecoat ironing the shirt she has bought for me to wear tomorrow. I watch her move the iron fluently over the collar, the yoke, the sleeves and the cuffs. There are damp patches under her arms and the faint smell of her sweat mixes with the steam from the iron. It reminds me of when my father still lived with us. The mornings I would get into their bed, under the cover, with the maroon-and-chocolate-colored leaves printed on it. How I would work myself into the gap between their backs, and lie there feeling safe in the commingled scents from their sleeping bodies. After he left my mother threw all their bedding out. The garbage sacks sat on the curb for three days before trashmen collected them. Last week I came home from school and found her asleep, face down on the mattress without any sheets, an incense stick burned to a stub on a saucer on the floor.

As my mother irons I practice the questions I've prepared for Bernstein, trying to inject some gravity into my voice. My mother pauses, the shining underside of the iron in her raised right hand, and tells me I need to work on my diction. She hesitates at the word, and I know it is because she is not certain it is the right one. If it means exactly what she thinks it means. I laugh and tell her that's funny, coming from her. But she pretends not to hear me. She picks up the remote control from the ironing board and flicks through the eight channels available. She turns up the sound on the television until it drowns out my voice. Walter Cronkite is introducing a report from Harrisburg five months on after the Pennsylvania leak. They are talking about the effect of a small dose of radiation on a fetus.

We both wake up on the couch, the plastic cover sticking to our faces, the digital clock flashing 1:38 a.m. "Bed, Christopher. Now. Big day tomorrow," my mother says. I walk down the hall to my bedroom and lie listening to the sound of the television for another hour or so. There are sirens, a car chase and gunshots, then a man with a deep voice talking to a woman who replies in husky monosyllables, whose conversation I cannot follow. Before I fall asleep I think about my mother and the time, at a burger joint she had taken me to in Mid-City, she told me my father once beat her so badly she passed blood in her urine for two days.

My mother is subdued at breakfast the next morning. She fills my glass to overflowing. I watch the orange juice run down over the images of the Kentucky Derby that decorate the sides. My mother insists on brushing my hair before I leave. I stand impatiently before the big mirror in the hallway, by the flashing statue of Our Lady. "Go get him, Chris," she tells me.

Bernstein has recently taken over the twenty-fourth floor of the City National Tower. I learn from the press pack I was sent in advance of our meeting that Bernstein Inc. have offices in Mayfair, Tokyo, and New York City. The afternoon the press pack arrived my mother and I knelt at the glass coffee table in the living room going over the glossy documents, pinning each one under the paperweights she has collected since I was a baby. When I was younger I was fascinated by the collection she had gathered from thrift stores and mail order over the years, but she would always keep them out of reach, away from me, on a glass shelf. I can remember a time in my early childhood when my highest desire was to hold one of the paperweights in my hands. In one the stamen of a white flower opens out, in another there is a swirl that looks like a breaking wave—they cast their green and blue light across the documents from Bernstein.

The concourse in front of the City National Tower is busy with black-suited office workers. Cherice is my first point of contact at the building. Dressed like a cop or some kind of paramilitary, she stands by the reception desk. I can smell Soul Glo in her hair. It reminds me of the girl in my class whose father was shot dead last year getting into his car after a shift at the post office in the Ambassador Hotel. She calls me Sugar and asks me who I'm here to see. I hand her my letter from Bernstein Inc. I notice the plastic window is torn and I suddenly feel ashamed I haven't taken better care of it.

Cherice tells me I need to make my way to the twenty-fourth floor, then asks if I know where that is. I shake my head. She walks me over to the bank of elevators and waits with me until one comes, our reflections blurred in the pitted steel doors. On the twenty-fourth floor the receptionist's name badge says "Hi! I'm Debbie." The skin on her face is sun-damaged, patches of brown pigment clustered under her eyes and down the sides of her mildly retroussé nose. The skin around the patches of pigment is opalescent. She is talking to someone on the telephone and looks at a point somewhere over my shoulder. I stand waiting for a pause in the conversation. She rolls her eyes as she talks and I notice how her mascara has gathered in broken clumps around her lower lashes—she wipes it away with the tip of her little finger. Eventually she pauses, covering the mouth of the receiver with her hand. I give her my letter. She looks at it, trapping the telephone between her ear and her shoulder, then asks me who gave it to me, as if the letter had been stolen from her without her knowing.

It's Tuesday in the second week of the summer vacation. My mother is watching *Jeopardy*. A high school administrator from Irvine and a textbook sales tepresentative from Santa Monica are taking on the reigning champion. He has so far won a total of $24,525. My mother is shaking her head in disbelief. It's sunny outside but the blinds in the living room are down so we can see the television. In a pan simmering on the front burner of the stove a chicken carcass is breaking apart. The fine bleached bones floating to the surface of the broth. We have the front door open and the ventilation fan on in the kitchen. A breeze, that is warm and smells of the fatty chicken flesh, is drifting through the room. The UPS man parks his van up outside the house.

Hearing the engine shutting down, I turn from the TV and watch the man in the brown uniform walk across the small, untended garden to our porch. He kicks away the newspapers in their plastic wraps from the path into the long grass. He knocks at the inside of the door frame and says he has a package for Mr. Lewkoski.

My mother flinches at my father's name. I get up from in front of the television. I walk to the door. The man in the brown uniform asks me if I am Mr. Lewkoski. I tell him, somewhat uncertainly, that I am. He hands me a large padded envelope with my name and address typed in capital letters on the label. He turns his clipboard to me and takes the chewed stub of a pencil from behind his ear. I attempt a signature then worry if I'm meant to tip him. But he just smiles and tells me to enjoy my day now.

As Debbie reads the letter, she coils a yellow cork-screw of hair around her index finger. She tells me to have a seat and then cautions me that Bernstein is a very busy man. I notice her eyebrows are tattooed onto her eyebrow arches; ditto a dark line around the circumference of her lips. My feet are hot. I want to slip off my Nikes and feel the cool of the tiles on my bare feet. Or better still slide across its polished surface in my tube socks. I imagine sliding along the office floor and Debbie's chagrin as she chases after me down the hallway in her stilettos.

I'm still sitting there when the office begins its lunch-hour migration down to the sandwich stores and restaurants around Pershing Square. The office empties out quickly and eventually even Debbie makes to leave. She stands and I watch her apply a ring of tangerine lipstick, delicately and with great care. She seems to enjoy the feel of the lipstick against her mouth, and pouts slightly as she judges her handiwork in a compact mirror. I think about the other kids in my class and wonder what they are doing now, and despite the hour and a half I have been waiting I feel lucky to be here in this world of adults. Before she leaves, Debbie tells me to help myself to water, gesturing to the cooler in the corner. I sit and listen to the phones ringing in the deserted office. I look over my questions for Bernstein and notice two thumb marks on the paper where I have been gripping it.

"Christopher?" The voice from above sounds like an expensive car moving slowly over gravel. I look up from my questions. I recognize Bernstein from the signed black and white photograph that was included in the fact pack. He is a mountainous man and wears a plaid suit. The jacket's wide shoulders emphasize his mass. The suit trousers come in tight at the waist, then flare out voluminously at the calf. He has a thick, reddish beard clipped to an even length all over. His hair is the same shade of reddish brown and, I notice, so close to the texture of his beard as to be almost identical. It is difficult to say for sure where one begins and the other ends. "Mr. Bernstein, sir," I say, rising to my feet.

I follow Bernstein through a warren of gray high-sided cubicles. There are photographs of families pinned inside some of them. In one a man stands with a boy next to Jack Youngblood at a Rams game. All three of them wear the number 85 jersey and smile into the camera with large, white, even teeth.

When we reach Bernstein's office he takes off his jacket. He asks me if I like it and opens the gray plaid to reveal the silk lining. "Oleg Cassini," he pronounces the name as a shaman might a shibboleth. He tells me it's from Cassini's signature collection and then, as an afterthought, that he's a personal friend. He drapes his jacket carefully over his tall-backed leather chair and then takes a seat behind his desk. The downtown skyline arrayed behind him. I wait in the doorway. He tells me to come in and that there must be a lot I want to ask as he saw I had some questions written down.

On his desk sits a matte snake-skin stationery set and a wooden cigar box with an ivory trim. He turns the box toward me with great ceremony, the way I've seen altar boys handle the offertory at the church my mother takes us to each Christmas and Easter, using the fingertips of both hands, and opens the lid. I hesitate, unsure how I should respond to his offer. He quickly spins the box back toward himself and tells me he's kidding. I watch him select a cigar, the outer skin made from a single tobacco leaf, rolling it between his thumb and forefinger, as he runs it between his upper lip and his nostrils, which flare as he inhales. I feel my ears begin to redden. The band on the cigar is the color of my mother's nail polish. It has a golden crown and above the crown the words "Juan Lopez." Bernstein lights it with a series of low, throaty puffs. He sits smoking in the large office filled with sunlight. He seems to enjoy his cigar and is in no hurry to talk. I look down at the questions. He exhales and, behind the smoke, raises his eyebrows and says, "Hoagie's stogie. Get it?"

Bernstein sends a mouthful of smoke up toward the grid of tiles in the suspended ceiling. He tells me my visit is due to a new member of his Public Relations team. How she suggested they get a local kid in from a school newspaper to counteract some of the smears his company has received in the press at what he calls a grassroots level. A photographer will be coming soon to take our picture. Bernstein turns his cigar toward himself. He taps the inch or so of compacted ash that has gathered at its tip into a cut-glass ashtray. I look at the wedge of ash, the gray layers and black seams curled in on each other, and I think of the men my mother has over to the house at night when I am in bed and she assumes that I am asleep. How the next morning the ashtray in the living room will be piled with cigarette butts, Newports, and sometimes Viceroys. Brands I know she does not smoke.

Bernstein looks into the raw orange embers of his cigar. He tells me his father was in the services, so he moved about a lot and that he spent a term at Venice High. And how when they asked my school to send over a list, he ran through it, saw my name and told Public Relations to get him in here. And here I am.

2

Tank man stands defiant in Tiananmen Square. I have graduated third in my class at Columbia's J-School and am nine months into a training contract at the Chicago *Sun Times*. I'm traveling to Los Angeles to interview Bernstein for the second time in my life. I've taken a week's leave from the paper to catch the Southwest Chief, forty-three hours across country. Evening is coming on but there is still a little light left in the sky. The horizon is dissected by telephone wires that run alongside the track. Their dark poles are flashing by. In the distance beyond the ochre sticks of corn stubble are three white farm buildings and a silver grain tower and because of the direction of the track they seem to be turning away slowly to my right.

My editor has promised me a full page if I can file my copy by next Friday. I'm sitting at a table in the observation car going through a folder of cuttings on the Bernstein case. So far he's refused to talk to anyone. It's a coup for me to get this hour with him. After six months on obituaries I was eventually seconded to the news desk to cover for a junior reporter who had shattered his spine when the car he was driving hit a tree on the way back from a bar in Bridgeport. I calculate it has taken almost twenty hours of phone calls to track Bernstein down and another five to set up and confirm the meeting. His people are specific about the date, place, and time. I figure I could use the week's leave prior to this meeting to brush up on the facts.

Somewhere between Lawrence and Topeka a blonde woman, who I guess is roughly my age, wearing black spectacles and carrying a sandwich wrapped in cellophane, asks if the seat next to me is free. She has an air of seriousness, of someone whose beauty is a distraction that she would shake if she could. I pull the pile of cuttings toward me. She sits down. I watch her unwrap the sandwich then carefully pick it apart. First the wheat bread, then the wilted strip of lettuce, the white meat of the chicken, which she prods at before tearing it into strips. She seems to have little appetite for the sandwich. The seats behind us in the observation car are occupied by a group of ladies in their sixties. They all wear sunglasses and hold their handbags on their laps with their thin hands, as they gaze out across Kansas.

I ask the girl in black spectacles if she is going all the way through. She tells me she is but only because she wasn't able to get a flight back to Los Angeles at such short notice. Then she tells me her name is Molly. I learn that she is training to be an attorney at John Marshall. When I ask her what's taking her back to California, she tells me her father is a dentist in Calabasas and she is visiting him. But that doesn't seem to tally with the speed of her departure from the city and I suspect there may be a man involved back in Chicago. Molly has a Superliner Roomette paid for on her father's Amex. I have a seat back in coach. She asks me about the cuttings and I explain about the Bernstein case and the charges the federal government are looking to bring against him and how it's funny as I actually met him, years ago, when I was at high school.

After a little over an hour of occasionally stilted, but not unpleasant conversation, Molly grows tired. I watch her working a finger under the rim of her glasses, until the insides of her eyelids grow red against her blue irises. I sense that I've lost her attention. I wish her good night as she makes back for her car. A few minutes later a retired Amtrak engineer takes up the empty seat. He offers me a beer, dislocating it with a twist from the plastic web of the four-pack he is carrying. We talk about the route the train will take through the night. He knows the stretch well and makes the journey, he tells me, at least twice a year, sometimes more, to visit a cousin in Brentwood who he fishes with. Then he tells me a story about arriving at the scene of an accident near Gallup, New Mexico, where a man had driven the family station wagon across a barricade. The man had survived and was standing by the wreckage of the car shaking his head when he got there. His wife and children were all killed on impact. Looking out at the night sky and the growing starlight he describes the scene inside the car to me in detail.

I don't see Molly again and pass an uncomfortable night back in my seat in coach. I wake around 2 a.m. and see a warehouse on fire in the distance. In the morning we arrive in Los Angeles and as we're leaving the train, Molly comes up to me on the platform and gives me her number. She tells me she'll look out for my piece and that if I'm free I should look her up when I'm back in Chicago.

"Christopher, right?" Bernstein holds the loaded pistol of his finger at me. We sit in a booth in the gloom of Cole's Pacific Electric Buffet. He bites into a pastrami french dip, the ruff of pink meat spilling from its edge. "One thing I need you to know," he tells me, "is that I'm going to fight this. All the way." He moves around his seat, zipping and unzipping his tracksuit top as he talks, glancing side to side as if on the lookout for photographers.

Bernstein tells me there is a lot he can't talk about. A lot of it would be unethical and inadvisable to discuss at this juncture. Over the course of the afternoon I fill three cassettes. An hour and a half into our conversation an aide comes over and tells us it's time to wrap it up. As I get up to leave Bernstein tells me there's really nothing to link the congressmen to those junk bonds. That if they want to defend his business from the regulators, that's their business. It doesn't make them corrupt, it doesn't make them crooks. And it doesn't mean he's not clean. He looks up from the remnants of his sandwich, then tells me the last piece on the school paper, that I did a good job. I ask him if he really read that. He tells me he reads all his press.

3

In squares across Belgrade thousands of angry Serbs are calling for Milošević to resign. I'm flying in from Washington, where for five years I have worked on the news desk at the *Post*, to interview Bernstein. Ten years now since I saw him last and twenty since that afternoon in the City National Tower. The plane is full. A toddler in the row in front has been crying ever since we hit a patch of rough air over Missouri. Her mother, who has alopecia, is unable to soothe her. I'm on my second Bloody Mary, the sachet of Clamato taking the edge off the warm vodka. Bernstein, according to his press release, is rebranding and bouncing back. It came through on the fax in the office a few weeks ago. Remember this asshole? Michael Naomi, a junior colleague, who I do not trust but who is the stepson of a former editor, said lifting the page to the air. I know that guy, I told him.

Bernstein isn't the real reason I'm in town. I was practically the only person in the office who remembered, or cared to remember, the case. It's my mother. I'm in town because of her. When the taxi drops me in Mar Vista, the driver turns around and tells me he recognizes me. He asks me if I ever played football. I say no, but he asks me again and tells me he's sure I did. I hand him two twenty-dollar bills and get out of the car.

The house is exactly as I remember it. My mother's things are everywhere, untouched, as if she just that minute stepped out to the Mini-Mart for a packet of Consulate. As I enter the house I have a vision of her standing on the porch the afternoon I got back from interviewing Bernstein for the first time. Over the years she accumulated more and more useless things. There are bags of fabric swatches and samples, stacks of videotapes labeled in her handwriting. There are three VCRs piled one on top of the other. That evening in her room I find a suitcase full of my clothes from childhood. In the end, my mother had amassed so much junk we stopped coming to the house when we would visit. Molly insisted. Instead we would take her and the kids to the IHOP on Sepulveda.

My mother's house will be sold at auction in two days' time. The realtor assures me it should reach close to the asking price. I will stay here to supervise the clearing out of all of her belongings. I wish there was something I could feel sentimental about. But it is as if in those last years alone in the house she tried to bury what was left of her life under all of these blankets, boxes, piles of old newspapers, empty orange tubes that held her prescriptions. When my mother got really sick we flew her out to Washington to be near us. Molly and the kids were happy to have her around. But it was rushed and the house in Mar Vista was left untouched. We would send her neighbor, a Korean woman with a large family, fifty dollars a month to check on the house. Molly and I talked of a second home but it was never practical.

I stand in the living room and look across at the neighbors. They are grilling large pieces of meat on the bone on a barbecue on the front lawn. I clear a space for myself on the sofa and pass the night watching reruns. I leave early the next morning to meet Bernstein.

Bernstein is operating out of a rental in the lobby of one of the old banks downtown. He is well liked by his neighbors. The unit next door sells chubby dolls in garish wedding dresses; the other, Chinese electronics. As he talks to me it's as if he is trying to convince himself of the pitch he has prepared.

Bernstein tells me Bio-Gas is the next big thing and that before long everyone is going to have a unit in their backyard like the one he is standing next to. As he speaks he taps down his mustache with a series of quick strokes. He tells me those who don't are going to be kicking themselves. We walk around the green dome. It looks like a child's idea of a UFO. As I inspect the machine Bernstein tells me that this place will change you. It was low security which meant he had lots of time to read. That was how he got on to this eco-kick. It's going to be big business, he says.

I ask him whose idea the press release was and he tells me one of the volunteers at the center he attends suggested it. She spent a year at Bernstein Inc. after college. He didn't remember her but she helped him draft it and even let him send it out from her office fax machine one evening after they closed. He rests his hand on the side of the machine and tells me she thought that his reputation might drum up a bit of extra business. I ask him if the design is his. He shakes his head and tells me he's just a kind of sales agent.

"I used to come down here as a kid," Bernstein says to me. "My old man, that term we lived in Venice, he loved to take me downtown to the movie theaters. The Belasco, the Cameo, the Globe. Some days he'd even take me out of class to go watch movies. He'd turn up in his army uniform and whisper something to the teacher, then he'd signal for me to come to the front of the class. Then we'd walk out together side by side. Neither of us smiling until we'd reached the car. We'd go watch a movie, and afterwards he'd walk me down here to buy an ice cream. Riddles were his thing, always coming with the riddles. The more it dries, the wetter it gets. What is it?" Bernstein looks at me impatiently. "I don't know," I say. "A towel," Bernstein snaps, then smiling asks, "What grows when it eats, but dies when it drinks? Fire," he tells me before I have time to answer. "You know your old man?" he asks. I shake my head. "Mine, he died when I was sixteen years old. The transporter plane he was in hit a cliff on Pali Kea Peak. Shouldn't even have been on that flight but he'd swapped with a buddy who was trying to get home to see his own son who was so sick with polio he'd had to be put in an iron lung. Back when I had money, I mean real money, I'd have given every cent to spend another hour with my old man. Every last single stinking cent just to hear another one of those dumb riddles."

At the entrance to the arcade I tell Bernstein I'll do what I can. If it doesn't run this time, it'll go on file or get farmed out to some local paper. People always need copy. I lie and turn my cell phone over in my hand, thumbing the keys. Bernstein thanks me, offering his hand. Then he says congratulations and I look at him, puzzled. That last piece you wrote, that profile for the *Sun Times*, it won some kind of award, right? he asks. I tell him it did but that was the only award I ever won, and it did little good as I've been passed over for promotion every year since arriving at the *Post*. He seems not to hear me. He offers me congratulations again. Then he gives me the thumbs-up, like a settler with nowhere left to go, planting a flag in the ground.

4

Michael Jackson's cadaver rests in the Staples Center. The skies outside our office are loud with helicopters from the networks. This morning my editor sent one reporter to gather quotes from the fans signing the condolence mural and had another follow the hearse down from the Forest Lawn Cemetery to see if he could get anything from the family. This was going to be my job but I made an excuse about needing to finish a cost analysis that our paper's new owners were making each of their acquisitions undergo. Just after midday I get the call that Bernstein is waiting for me in the lobby.

Shortly after I arrived at the *Downtown News*—the *Post* had let me go and Molly had wanted to move home to be closer to her father who had early-onset dementia—I was sent to cover the opening of a new facility for the homeless. I stood behind a city councilor as he gave a speech standing on a hastily erected podium. I recognized Bernstein at the far edge of the crowd, standing next to a man in army fatigues who was asleep in a wheelchair. He was wary of me at first. Then I told him we'd met, a few times in fact. I asked him about himself. He told me he was living in a single-occupancy hotel on Spring Street. At night he hears people in the room above plotting to kill him. They are planning to slice out his eyes with a box cutter, then dump his butchered body in plastic bags in the LA river. He says he has hard evidence of this. I told him he was welcome to come over to the office for lunch sometime and that all he needed to do is ask for me at reception.

I see him as the elevator doors open. Standing uneasily in the lobby. His gray hair falls lank around his face. There are broken blood vessels, the color of an eggplant, under his right eye, that fade to yellow in a long smear. His nails are brown. He wears combat pants and a dated-looking jacket. I wave from the elevator. "Hey man," he says, his voice strung out, soft and low. "Come on up," I tell him as I hold the elevator doors open.

Janine has laid the food out across the table in the meeting room. A pizza, paper plates, two bottles of Coca-Cola and a pile of napkins left over from a lunch my boss threw last week. It looks like a five-year-old's party. You're a saint, I say, then I ask how long we have before our editor gets back from lunch. I watch her leave, then close the door to the meeting room. I tell Bernstein we have pizza this week and that I hope that works for him. It takes a moment for my words to register through the haze. "Pizza, yeah, thanks, man," he says. I ask him if he wants to take a shower, and putting my hand on his shoulder, I say I've only got an hour this week. It's like talking down a line long distance.

I show Bernstein through to the shower my editor's predecessor at the paper had installed and which the current editor allows the few of us who sometimes cycle to work to use. I turn it on for him and the white cubicle fills with steam. As I wait, I stand over my desk and delete a string of e-mails. After Bernstein has showered and dressed, I go back into the restroom and push the used towels toward the laundry hamper with my foot. We sit at the meeting table and look out across the street.

I could give him the statistics: 198 murders this year so far, how even our mild winter will see a spike in morbidity in the people who live on the streets, how living rough here will take on average 36 percent off your life expectancy. I could tell him all of this. I could offer him the house I grew up in in Mar Vista. The house my mother got sick in after years of living alone and hoarding boxes of junk. The house where we never visited her enough and when it came to the day of the auction did not fetch its reserve price and after which I could not bring myself to sell. The house I sometimes take women I meet in bars back to when it's between tenants. I could offer him this. And if he promised to stay clean and off the booze, I could probably find him work and maybe get that rattle in his chest, which gets worse week by week, looked at by a specialist I know.

I could tell him how after I met him that day in 1979, my mother was so proud when I got home that night that she cried. And how I saw then her response as a poverty of ambition and how it galled me. Or how when he was in prison I thought of visiting once or writing to him but did neither. Or how the piece I wrote about the Bio-Gas franchise that he ran out of the rental in the old bank downtown for a few months in 1999 eventually ran in the *Askov*

*American* in Minnesota, and the *Clay County Leader* in Henrietta, Texas. But only after I'd contacted their editors directly. Or how when I lost my job at the *Post* and we decided to move back west to be near Molly's father, I had often thought about Michael Hogan Bernstein and had hoped that I might one day run into him. How I had rehearsed what I might say to him, until it became a game I would play. But I don't tell him any of this and I never have. Not all the weeks he's been coming up to the office to eat lunch with me.

We sit in silence with the pizza between us. I look down at the blistered dough. He takes a bite, chews it slowly, then sips from a red party cup full of warm Coca-Cola. The plastic cup trembling as he brings it to his lips. I tell him I like his jacket. Yeah, it's real nice, he says. Then, like he's recalling some language he doesn't quite understand, says, "Oleg Cassini." He shows me the label, hanging from the frayed lining. His eyes brighten for a moment. "He was a friend of mine, you know, a close personal friend," he says. Then he pauses. "Just like you, Christopher, just like you."

## Rambla Pacifico

The white fins glistened on Lindberg's Pontiac Bon-
neville as he drove along Rambla Pacifico. Glancing
from the road he saw a stray dog dragging its hind-
quarters through a grove of cypresses. The wires
between the telephone poles sagged as if melting
under the California sun. Lindberg shifted in his
seat, the new leather creaking as he squinted through
the windshield at the numbers of the mailboxes to
his left, looking out for the address he had scrib-
bled on a paper napkin. On the radio a newscaster
was announcing that an airliner had hit the water a
hundred miles off Galway Bay. Lindberg spotted the
number he was looking for and swung the long frame
of the Pontiac across the opposing highway, bumping
up the dirt track, red dust rising in clouds around the
bright white automobile.

Jesus Porfirio was stacking boxes out back when he
heard the car pull up. He wiped his palms on his apron
and walked into the store just in time to see a tall man
stooping to enter. The man held a brown fedora above

his heart. As the sound of the ringing bell spent itself, Jesus turned down the volume on the radio on the counter. The tall man walked toward him.

"Hear about the crash?" he said, casting a finger wearily at the radio as one might cast a fly rod after a long day fishing on the river. He took a handkerchief from his breast pocket and dabbed at the beads of sweat gathered on his forehead.

"Terrible business. Ninety-nine dead. Just dropped out of the air."

The voice was urbane, brittle, East Coast. He reminded Jesus of Puller, the major he served under in the 1st. "Chesty" Puller who took two bullets from a sniper on Guadalcanal. The man in front of Jesus looked like a scarecrow, too thin for the broad beam of his shoulders: as Puller had looked in the pictures in the *Army Gazette* when they pinned the purple heart to his chest.

"Can you imagine it," the man continued, "some poor bastard's job to pull all those corpses from the water." He slowly shook his head at the terrible tragedy, as if he might have done something to avert it. "They'll be picking pieces of those bodies from the beaches for weeks."

Jesus nodded and placed his fists on the wooden counter. A fan rattled in the corner of the store. There was a pause. Then the tall man changed the timbre of the conversation.

"Arthur Lindberg," he said, extending his hand, a smile curling on his thin lips. "I was told you might be able to help us?"

"He says he is no longer in that line of work," the fat boy with caramel skin, puffing at his inhaler, said to Lindberg as the three of them sat on upturned egg crates in the backyard of the grocery store. The boy swatted at his friends as they beckoned him back to their game of stickball. Hands folded on his lap, Jesus stared at Lindberg, expressionless, as if he was cut from Sierra brown stone.

"Please explain to Senor Porfirio that this is a matter of some urgency. If money is the object . . ."

In sonorous rapid Spanish the boy addressed Jesus. Jesus shook his head.

"Well, that leaves us at an impasse," Lindberg said, twisting the signet ring on his pinkie up to the knuckle, exposing a white band of skin.

"Tell you what, sport. Give this to Mr. Porfirio. Tell him to be in touch if he changes his mind. We're very keen to employ his services."

The boy nodded disinterestedly and passed the card to Jesus.

In the store Lindberg, still shaky from last night's booze, hadn't known what to make of the man standing in front of the shelves that held enough tins to stock a nuclear bunker. This was Jesus Porfirio? This was the man he had driven two hours through the desert to come and see? A stocky storekeeper with a downturned mouth and a pudgy, impassive face that looked like it had been formed by a cookie cutter? The small man with the apron tied tightly below his breastbone, this was the Beast of the 1st? This was the man who had taken a Japanese blockhouse single-handed the day "Manila" John Basilone was blown into a thousand pieces by a 75 mm round above the airfield at Iwo Jima? The day they said the bodies of Japanese servicemen were piled so high one GI mistook them for sandbags and slumped down against them to flick through his copy of *Life* magazine.

Chase Labouchere had been there the day Basilone died or so he liked to boast. It was a story Chase would tell, dressed in one of his loud Hawaiian shirts, his vermilion slacks, propping up the bar in the Lamu Lounge. His feminine mouth twitching as he spoke, his eyes with their dark lashes darting from side to side, a face at odds with his prematurely balding head. Lindberg had never liked Chase, the way he used to brag about the war, to talk about himself in the third person. Boasting that his company commander had been so impressed by his accuracy at four hundred yards (learned, he said, killing bucks east of the mainline Mississippi River) that he had paid for Chase's mother to ship out his hunting rifle. Chase would mime fixing the telescopic sight, pulling back the bolt, loosing a round at the unsuspecting head of some salesman or honeymooner who stood talking by the piano at the far end of the bar. Then all the cocktail-sipping ladies of Palm Springs would break into laughter as Chase blew a cloud of cigarette smoke from the imaginary barrel. The Old Man had hired Chase a few months before Lindberg had arrived. Lindberg heard a rumor from some of the girls in the typing pool that Chase had been an orderly during the war at a convalescent hospital in Georgia and had never seen active service.

When Lindberg's firm had folded, he had taken up the role of foreman on this new project out in the desert. A golden handshake from across the states. He came across the small ad in the back of a trade journal. "Major Building Project. Help wanted. Excellent rates. Experience a must." He'd weighed it up before calling, pacing his tiny apartment on Avenue C, grimacing at the empty pints of Scotch that littered his floor like spent shell casings in a gun placement, the Puerto Rican portion of Manhattan loud outside his window. The divorce was almost through, Angelica and the girls were up in Maine. He'd heard that she had been seen out at a social with the head of the local Rotary Club. As he paced the apartment he thought about those last weeks in the office, only Loretta kept on at the front desk. Her scent catching at his throat each time he walked by: "Ambush," The Tender Trap—A Romance in Every Bottle, the billboards proclaimed. Those afternoons of enforced idleness spent flicking through yachting magazines, staring at the fifty-four-foot cruising ketch he had once coveted but now knew he would never own. A spectator looking down from the bleachers as his life crumbled around him. Then the repo men arriving to take away the office furniture, right down to the ship in a bottle that had been a wedding gift from Angelica and had sat for two decades on his desk.

It had been hard to tell exactly when and how Lindberg QS had gone to the dogs. When Lindberg flunked out in his second year of architecture at Cornell, his father had insisted he take up a profession. He signed up to a series of night-school classes, hiding his attendance from the crowd from his prep school he was running around Manhattan with at the time. After four years he qualified as a quantity surveyor and after two, working for a small firm in Delaware, he set up on his own. Business had flourished, a steady stream of work channeled his way by Angelica's father. But when her father had retired from his position in the city, work had been harder to come by. "Death by a thousand cuts," Lindberg overheard Angelica telling a friend on the telephone one evening when he had come home late, half-drunk. Shocked at first to see him, the lipstick-red receiver cradled at her shoulder, she held his gaze as she explained in detail the intricacies of their predicament. He felt tiny standing before her, as a juvenile might before a judge as he was passing sentence and listing explicitly the crimes of which he was about to be convicted. Now, fifty-three and divorced, Lindberg had been overseeing the building of a new hotel in the desert. An eternity of time to drink his way through. A new car, a rented room in an upscale motel in Palm Springs and, as of 9:30 p.m., the daughter of his employer missing, feared dead.

Lindberg was sitting on the edge of his bed when he heard the news. Stripped to his boxer shorts, his undershirt hanging loose from his wilting, hairless body, running his finger around the indent his garters had left above his calf. It was a hot night and the door to his room was open. He watched a shining black vinyl disc rotate on his Dansette Deluxe. Mario Lanza was singing opera.

"*Vesti la giubba*," Lindberg closed his eyes and mouthed the words.

"I don't know it," said a voice, "you got any Chuck Berry?"

Chase stood in the doorway, winking as he raised his hip flask to Lindberg, who exhaled heavily.

"I'm meeting Lynette and Francine at the Rose," Chase said.

"Thanks. I'll pass."

Lindberg hated Chase's intrusions, his frequent offers of hospitality. But when the bar called him back, tired of drinking alone in his room or buzzed from a quarter pint of Scotch, the liquor lending him the sensation he had something to offer the world again, he would find himself in the vicinity of Chase Labouchere. Lindberg couldn't say for certain what Chase's job involved. He was a fixer of some sort. The guy the Old Man sent to take some clerk in the building regulations' office out for a steak dinner, or pass an envelope to a city councilor. Mostly these days Chase seemed to spend his time trying to track down Adella. Adella Smart, the Old Man's daughter. Adella of the coal-black eyes and cinnamon skin. Adella of the mesmeric sashay. Adella whose grandmother had been the first Latina in a motion picture. Descended from Cortés or so the Old Man liked to boast. Adella Smart, twenty-one last September. Adella who loved jazz and jazzmen and Christ knew what else. Adella who would make the air feel heavy in your lungs when she walked through her father's office. Adella whose fragrant specter rose up in Lindberg's mind as he lay in his undershirt and boxer shorts in his single bed, head reeling from the malt, his member limp in his hand.

"Are you sure?"

"Positive."

"I can't tempt you?"

"No."

"Francine thinks you're a dish."

"Really, Chase, I'm tired. Let me go to bed."

"Well, all the more for Chasey."

He bowed at Lindberg, raising his hip flask as the needle crackled to static against the paper label of the record. There was a screech of tires on asphalt outside, then the sound of a car slamming into garbage pails and a long groan from its horn. A dog began to bark. Chase looked down from the first-floor balcony of the motel and saw Nicky, the office errand boy, sprinting across the parking lot toward Lindberg's room, his tanned face visible against the darkness.

"Slow down, kid," Chase shouted from the doorway.

As Nicky reached the room Chase laid his palm on the boy's chest.

"Sir . . ." The boy could barely catch his breath.

"Mr. Lindberg, sir, it's Adella," he stuttered.

"Ah jeez, what's she done this time?" asked Chase.

"Mr. Lindberg, Mr. Smart would like you to come to his house immediately."

"It's late," Chase said, tapping his watch.

"Something has happened to Adella."

The Old Man was based out in the desert but was buying up land in Los Angeles. He had a big residential development under way up in the Highlands, two hotels under construction in Palm Springs and a plan to run a monorail up Mount San Jacinto. He lived in what had once been a pink-walled finca out toward the mountains. He'd shown Lindberg around the place the weekend he arrived from New York. The Old Man had torn down the original farmhouse and erected a low-rise, sleek-lined, geometrical building. When Lindberg and Chase arrived the Old Man was pacing around the courtyard, anxious as a bridegroom before a rose arch on his wedding day. He escorted the men into the dining room, closing the heavy wooden doors behind him. At the head of the table, Lindberg at his right, Chase hovering behind nodding, the Old Man outlined the facts of Adella's disappearance. Lindberg listened but only heard those words the Old Man chose to emphasize:

"Signs of scuffle . . . we *think* is blood . . . mother's jewels . . . no note, yet . . ."

And then with emphasis that focused Lindberg's attention, "Bas Rodriguez found her door kicked clean off its hinges . . ."

The Old Man left a pause at the end of his outline.

"The question is, gentlemen, how do we resolve this situation?"

Lindberg noticed the Old Man's hands were trembling.

"For reasons I don't need to go into here, I'm loath to involve the police, at least not at this stage. Not until we know what's what."

Lindberg sat tense in the silence of the wood-paneled, windowless room whose four walls were hung with sporting prints.

"There's a lot of this about," Chase said, moving toward the sideboard and the silver tray that held a glass decanter.

"Last month I heard of a girl, Adella's age, getting snatched down in Gardena." Chase paused, then with the forced gravity of a TV anchor added, "They found her body part eaten by dogs behind a Dumpster in Nevada a few blocks from her father's casino."

Lindberg looked down. His face was reflected darkly in the polished mahogany table. He covered it over with his hand.

"But I know someone who might be able to help," Chase said, pouring himself a generous tumbler of Scotch.

"Yes?" the Old Man said. Lindberg detected the note of frailty in his voice. This was the person Lindberg had watched only last week manhandle out of his office two Cuban businessmen who, having run casinos under Batista, had flown up from Miami to make an uninvited cash offer on one of his hotels. The Old Man had taken the shorter by the neck of his shirt, then twisted the arm up the back of his taller associate. His face flushed crimson as he pushed them out into the corridor and down past the rows of typists, who, although shocked, continued with their work.

"Yeah, I ain't got a number but I got an address," Chase said. "I ever tell you about Jesus Porfirio?" he looked over at Lindberg.

"Maybe."

"Before I took one in the shoulder I was with him in the 1st. Truth be told my brother Alphonse knew him better. They saw action together at Iwo Jima. He helped a friend of mine find someone a while back."

"OK," said Lindberg.

"You're suggesting Mr. Porfirio might be able to help us?" asked the Old Man.

The Old Man was on his feet now, hands clasped behind his back staring vacantly at a framed poster for a boxing match that had taken place fifty years ago. It advertised the "Battle of the Little Gladiators" as "Volcano" Corbert took on "Fighting Dick" Hyland, twenty rounds, straight rules under the auspices of the Palace Athletic Club, Salt Lake City. Lindberg remembered the Old Man once pointing out his own name in tiny print listed on the undercard for the fight.

"Yes, I think he might," Chase said, walking across to Lindberg.

He placed a hand on Lindberg's shoulder and leaning down whispered, "I'd go myself but . . ." He looked over at the Old Man, "I need to be here for Mr. Smart. I'm his right hand."

"Sure," Lindberg said wearily, "sure you are."

The drive was long. The men had decided to wait until the next morning in case any contact was made by the people who had taken Adella. If not, Lindberg would be sent to find Jesus Porfirio. Shortly after this had been decided Chase had headed into Palm Springs to see if he could unearth any information. Though Lindberg expected this meant him sitting in a bar somewhere boasting to Lynette and Francine about the evening's events and his role in initiating the hunt for Adella. The Old Man made Lindberg sit up until 2 a.m. with him, working their way through a bottle of Black Label and a box of bad cigars. Lindberg had watched the Old Man move through several moods as anger ebbed to open despair, which had itself eventually given way to an old fighter's sentimentality. The Old Man yelling up every so often from the cast-iron table the gardeners usually sat around in their lunch hour for Nicky, who was up on the balcony with the gramophone, to change the record. As the night wore on the Old Man had become weepy, describing Adella as his jewel, his baby girl and other epithets not quite in keeping with the young woman Lindberg knew. As they sat at the table Lindberg heard the songs the Old Man romanced her mother to, the song they played at their wedding and all the other saccharine melodies he swore Adella loved as much as he did. As the Old Man talked Lindberg thought back to the first Christmas party. How he had danced with Adella around the huge fir tree that stood at the far edge of the swimming pool, now strung with fairy lights and giant silver baubles. "You're light on your feet, old timer," she whispered as they waltzed between the lounge chairs. Lindberg had laughed and leaned her over his arm then pulled her up into a twirl, her ruched skirt billowing out as she spun. When the song ended they sat together on the corners of a pair of sunloungers. She had taken two cigarettes from the top of her dress and, lighting them both at the same time, passed one across to Lindberg. He had taken a shallow drag— as he did, he saw that his hand was shaking. He switched the cigarette clumsily into his other hand, then slid the shaking hand under his leg, where it began to sweat against the slats of the lounge. Adella pulled a shred of tobacco from the commissure of her lips, then tipped her head back, exposing the sweep of her slender brown neck to the sunlight.

"What do you dream about?" Adella asked.

"What do I dream about?"

"Yeah, what do you dream about?" she asked again, narrowing her eyes, rolling a thin blue plume of smoke from between her lips.

"The past. I suppose," Lindberg said, "I dream of what's gone. Sometimes I dream of my children."

Adella nodded as if she understood the dreams Lindberg had, as if she knew what it was to live so far away, to miss their love, to wake after dreaming their faces and think himself unworthy of it. She studied Lindberg, tracing his outline with her smoke as she exhaled. She ran the tip of her tongue across her top lip. Glanced away across the pool, then turned back and looked straight at Lindberg.

"You ever dream of me?" she asked.

"Of you?"

"Of me."

There was a pause. Voices from the far side of the party filled up the silence.

"Of course," Lindberg said. At which Adella broke into laughter and before Lindberg knew it, she was up on her feet gripping him by his bony wrist and pulling him up from the lounge, the unfinished cigarette hanging from her soft mouth.

"Get up," she said out of the corner of her mouth, "get up and dance with me, old timer." The cigarette now delicately held between her ring finger and her pinkie, "I love this song."

Later he had seen her leave, hurrying toward a parked car. He was standing at the window in the bathroom where he had gone in search of aspirin after a twinge from the ulcer an expensive physician on the Upper East Side had diagnosed several years ago. Harry Belafonte's voice echoed around the party as Lindberg watched the car that held Adella pull away.

When Jesus Porfirio had refused to help, and at a loss as to what his next move should be, Lindberg had driven off down the dirt track and pulled into a turnout where he sat for five minutes, fingers at his temples as the engine idled over. He imagined the Old Man's wrath if he returned empty-handed, having failed to enlist the help of Jesus Porfirio. How Chase would linger in the background some-where slowly shaking his head. In the stifling late afternoon heat Lindberg began to feel drowsy, as he often had sitting behind the piles of ledgers and accounts at his desk in the last days of Lindberg QS. Back then sleep had been the answer when it was too early in the day to legitimately head to the bar. Here on Rambla Pacifico with no office blinds to lower, he pulled his fedora down over his eyes. Lindberg welcomed the soft exigencies of sleep and that long shot, that dumb but irresistible gamble, that waking might provide some answer to his predicament.

When Lindberg woke it was dusk. Something had pulled him from his dream. It was the dream he had continued to have even after he had moved out to the desert. The one where he was locked in his office in Manhattan alone as the building burned down around him, flames rising against the glass of his office door, the lettering of his name slowly peeling away. On opening his eyes, the first thing Lindberg saw was the sky over the Pacific, striated pink and violet. Then came the rap on the window. Jesus stood there. Lindberg noticed he was still wearing his apron. He was carrying an aluminium sandwich box. Lindberg wound down the window.

"I make some calls. I'm gonna help you. This is what it cost."

Jesus slipped a piece of paper through the gap in the window.

In the roadside diner the waitress refilled their cups. It was dark now and from their booth they could see the lights of traffic moving along the Pacific Coast Highway.

"So that's all we know," Lindberg said, fanning his hands out like a croupier. Then in a hectoring voice that reminded him of his own father and that he immediately regretted, "She was running around with some pretty disreputable characters."

Jesus turned the sugar dispenser's glass sides in his small hands.

"*Claro.*"

He lifted his sandwich box on to the table and retrieved from within a list of names.

"This," he said, tapping the sheet, "are the persons we need to visit."

The first address was a mansion in Upper Bel-Air where ornate gates and dense foliage hid the residences of the wealthy members of the country club and recently founded Presbyterian Church. The road leading to its entrance was lined with expensive automobiles parked at awkward angles. There was bunting strung across the wrought-iron gates between the two tall stone pillars that marked the entrance to the driveway. As they approached the guard at the entrance nodded to Lindberg. Jesus stared ahead along the driveway.

"This the place?" Lindberg asked out of the corner of his mouth.

"This the place," Jesus confirmed as Lindberg brought the Pontiac to a stop on the gravel turning circle that surrounded the fountain in front of the doorway.

"You wait for me here."

In the rearview mirror Lindberg saw Jesus talking to a white-coated waiter carrying a silver salver, who pointed him in the direction of the kitchen. Lindberg watched Jesus disappear behind the house.

"Darling, are you here for cocktails?"

Lindberg looked up from the driver's seat. A sunburned blonde, wearing a taffeta dress with a square neck and white gloves, was smiling down at him. She opened his door and held out her hand.

"You must be a friend of Genie? Am I right? I'm right, aren't I? Any friend of Genie is a friend of mine. Come on in or we'll miss all the fun!"

Lindberg hesitated.

"Come on, honey! Don't be shy."

Before he knew it the sunburned blonde's hand was on his wrist and Lindberg had been led into the busy ballroom. A band was playing in the corner. She handed him a drink, tapping her foot to the rhythm of the music. Lindberg sipped the cocktail from the chilled glass where three oversize olives skewered by a plastic shard left an oily sheen on the surface. It tasted good, it tasted of those summers with Angelica before the girls were born, when they would take his father's skiff around the bay from the Nyack Boat Club and end the day with a cocktail on the veranda looking out on to the Hudson River Palisades.

"You should try their Manhattans. They shake a mean Manhattan," the sunburned blonde said. She then turned and greeted her friend, a butch woman a decade or so older with sad, Slavic eyes and a brown bonnet of hair.

"Myrtle, darling, this is Mr. . . ." The sunburned blonde paused. "Why, I don't believe I got your name."

"Lindberg."

"This is Mr. Lindberg," then turning to her friend, "friend of Genie."

"Any friend of Genie is a friend of ours," they said in unison.

Lindberg raised his glass.

Tensely sipping his martini, Lindberg watched the women dance. Their shapes moving around the white room seemed to belong to a land of the young from which Lindberg was permanently exiled. Although the dresses and movements had changed, it brought back the memories of the dances he had attended in Nyack. A man with slicked-back black hair was swinging the sunburned blonde around his hips. Lindberg watched as she clamped her legs around his upper thighs, then he swung her up, almost vertical, above him, revealing a black garter belt beneath her taffeta dress. The party was heating up. More and more guests seemed to be arriving now. Lindberg was buffeted from side to side as they entered the ballroom. The snatches of their conversations came at him loud and distorted. In the swirl of noise he tried to steady himself and focus in on a single sound. He picked out the laughter of a large man in black tie who feigned throwing a punch at his pal on the dance floor. Lindberg began to feel dizzy.

He took another long pull from his martini, the sap of panic rising as he thought of Adella.

As the music from the band grew louder, Lindberg watched the drummer, a bald-headed black man in a white tuxedo, pursed lips purple at their edges, tapping his brushes at the snare drum in its shining silver surround. The hiss of the snare began to overwhelm him. As Lindberg looked away the faces in the room began to spin and warp as if he were on a carousel that was gradually gaining speed. The way Angelica, a migrainer since childhood, had once described the onset of a severe attack, the type that would see her laid up in bed for the best part of the week, the girls growing fractious and restive as she absented herself from family life. Just when Lindberg thought he would have to elbow through the crowd and push his way outside for air, he glanced over his shoulder and saw Jesus standing at the entrance to the ballroom. Lindberg set down his glass and raised two fingers in acknowledgment. He hurried through the mass of bodies toward him.

"Oh, Mr. Lindberg," called the sunburned blonde, who had seen him leaving. But Lindberg pretended not to hear as the crowd closed behind him.

The bright notes of an alto sax reached Lindberg and Jesus as they stood on the gravel turning circle where they had left the car. Lindberg was pale and leaned for a moment against the hood of the Pontiac. He brought his handkerchief up to his mouth.

"My friend say we gotta go see someone else," Jesus said.

"OK," said Lindberg. Jesus noticed Lindberg was paler than when he had left him in the car earlier. A thin sheen of sweat on his face, like a waxwork replica of the man who had come to his store earlier in the day.

"You want me to drive?" Jesus asked.

"Thank you, no. It's just a little hot in there is all."

"*Claro*," Jesus said, "so now we need go to Long Beach."

Lindberg and Jesus drove the newly opened section of Interstate 5 toward Long Beach. The dizziness and nausea that had afflicted Lindberg in the cramped ballroom had lifted now. He let his focus fall on the white lines on the road as they slipped by at the side of the car.

"So what are your people telling you?" he asked Jesus, attempting to establish some sense of control or at least a cursory understanding of what was going on.

Jesus seemed not to hear Lindberg's question but a few moments later, as they passed a series of boarded-up and part-demolished houses, said softly and with what sounded to Lindberg like real sadness, "They just tear it all down." Jesus was looking out of the window to what was once Boyle

Heights, the section of the east side that had been razed to the ground to make way for the freeway. Lindberg remembered hearing a Latina attorney on the radio complain that the newly completed freeway had put a hole in the heart of a community that had been there since Los Angeles had been under Spanish dominion. Under arc lights a mechanical digger was clawing at the wall of a house. Inside they saw a Formica table with four chairs around it as if the occupants might return at any time.

When they arrived in Long Beach Jesus directed Lindberg to the forecourt of a Union Oil gas station. A torn poster on a billboard outside advertised its "Grand Opening" three years earlier. It was dark out and when Jesus left the car to go and find his contact, Lindberg pressed down the button on the passenger door. In the locked Pontiac Lindberg felt that sense of anxiety return. A static sweat prickling down his arms and hands, the growing conviction that each stop they made left Adella closer to danger. Unless it was already too late. The thought summoned an image of blanket blackness, the black of the woods at the back of their house and the skies he had looked up at as a child through his father's telescope. He would have to call the Old Man soon and update him. Through the windshield Lindberg watched an emaciated black woman, her hair in rollers, as she stood rocking back and forth by the phone booth on the gas station forecourt, shouting into the receiver then slamming it against the corner of the booth. He watched Jesus give the woman a wide berth as he returned to the car a few minutes later carrying a brown paper bag. They would have to wait, he told Lindberg; according to the girl at the register the person Jesus was looking for was not there.

They sat in silence in the Pontiac. Lindberg watched cars come and go with no idea of who or what they were waiting for. Occasionally he would look across to Jesus as drivers alighted to pay for their gas. Jesus sat implacable as ever. As they waited, the emaciated woman remained enraged at the phone booth. After a few minutes, a stooped man in his fifties wearing chinos and a stained undershirt approached her. Lindberg and Jesus watched as he wrestled the phone from the woman. He grabbed her by the wrist, then struck her across the face with the back of his open hand. The woman ducked and tried to shield herself with her free arm. But now the man struck her again, the blow this time landing on the back of her head, sending one of her pink plastic rollers spinning off across the forecourt. Lindberg looked across to Jesus who stared out at the scene as if he were watching a movie at a drive-in theater. As the man jerked her away from the booth, the woman began spitting then clawing at his face. The man turned, feigning once then twice, before bringing his hand down on her. This time as he made contact the woman collapsed and was dragged along for a few yards. Eventually she refused to get to her feet. In a pool of light on the edge of the forecourt, Lindberg saw the man kick her in the ribs. It seemed to Lindberg like the unthinking brutality farmers might use on their livestock or slaughter men at the doors to an abattoir.

"Shouldn't we help?" he asked.

"No," Jesus said. "We gotta wait here."

"But what if . . ."

"We gotta wait," Jesus said, more firmly this time.

The pair disappeared from view but Lindberg heard the woman's voice cursing until finally her shouting was canceled out by the sound of an ambulance heading in the opposite direction.

There was silence on the forecourt now. The handset swung by its cord from the booth. The men watched it lose momentum until it finally came to a stop. As they focused on the stilled receiver, Jesus began to speak.

"After we get home, in '45, a kid from my unit, Cooper, invites me drinking. Calls my momma's house. Sure, why not, I say. He was a quiet kid. We never talked much." Jesus paused and, reaching down into the paper bag he had returned with earlier, passed a bottle of beer across to Lindberg.

"But we seen a lot of action together," Jesus continued, "places you don't think you're gonna leave alive. He comes and gets me in this rusted pickup. We drive around a couple of hours. It's a hot night. We put away a lot of liquor between us, talking about the old times. Then he takes me to this bar he knows out by the ocean in Santa Monica. The place was full of sailors. We drink a couple of beers then he says we maybe should go down to the beach. I'm thinking to look for girls, you know?"

It was strange to see Jesus so talkative. Lindberg nodded for him to continue his story, then took a pull on the bottle of beer.

"There's a big moon like a searchlight up there. 'You saved my life,' Cooper says to me." Jesus chuckled remembering this. He opened his own bottle of beer now and took a pull.

"Cooper stands so close I can hear him breathing and see the stars all reflected in his eyes. Then I look down. Know what I see?"

Lindberg shrugged.

"Two guys screwing in the sand, arms and legs all twisted up, panting like they're animals." Jesus shook his head reliving the shock.

"I think of Cooper and me in that foxhole, times I woke up with him lying next to me, I think it's for to keep warm? Man, I get mad."

Lindberg watched the expression drain from Jesus's face.

"It just comes down on me, I pick up this piece of driftwood from the sand, start swinging it down on top of those guys. Like on TV when you see the hunters going at those seals. Nothing could stop me. Nada." Jesus chuckled as he recalled the scene on the moonlit beach. He wiped his hand across his mouth.

"I remember there was singing and the sound of a guitar from a fire down the sand. Then the singing stop and these guys with no shirts on come running over shouting at me."

Lindberg nodded and tried not to blink.

"So I swing the wood and one goes down, BAM! and then the other. Hit him so hard the wood snapped in my hand. Then two more guys come at me but I lay them out this time with my fists. Two shots to the face without even thinking about it. Then I pull one of them into me and take a bite right out of his ear. And now I'm screaming into the dark: 'Who else wants to fuck with Jesus Porfirio?'"

Lindberg watched the veins thickening in Jesus's neck as he spoke.

"Do you," Lindberg paused, "do you think you killed them? With the driftwood, I mean?"

"Nah. Takes more than you think to kill a man. I mean to really hurt someone." Jesus gestured with the neck of the bottle toward the phone booth where the emaciated woman had been dragged away.

Lindberg thought about this for a moment. "What did Cooper do?"

"Cooper? He just stands there crying like a little girl who lost her dog. 'Gimme the keys,' I say. When I walk back up the beach there's all this shouting. Suddenly the other guys get brave when my back turned, *claro*? But I just walk back to the pickup."

Lindberg nodded.

"I drive it back to my momma's house. We use it for a couple of weeks. Run errands, take my sisters' kids to the beach one afternoon. Then one day Cooper calls, all nervous. Asks if he can come get the car."

Lindberg held Jesus's gaze.

"'Sure,' I say. So he come with his mother, this old bear in her church bonnet, who just stands there shaking her head as he walks up the drive." Jesus broke into a smile.

"We was all laughing so loud."

Lindberg nodded, unsure what to make of the story as a green pickup truck pulled up on the forecourt.

"Here we go," said Jesus, setting down his beer on the car floor. He got out of the car and followed a thin man in dungarees into the gas station. Lindberg watched the two men talking. As he spoke to Jesus the thin man thumbed the buckles on his dungarees, rocking back and forth on his heels. From the car it was hard for Lindberg to gauge the tone of the conversation. After a few minutes the men emerged onto the forecourt. The thin man held out a limp hand to Jesus and, turning to his right, spat on the tarmac. They shook on something, then Jesus returned to the car, passing himself through the gap between the two red gas pumps.

"Yeah. She's alive," he said. "So now we get some sleep. We got to meet someone tomorrow."

Lindberg turned the key in the ignition.

"There's a motel across the street. We go there," Jesus told him.

Lindberg washed his face in the sink. He stared for a moment at the haggard mask that met his gaze in the cracked bathroom mirror: the skin on his neck sagging, the patches of hair at the edges of his throat that he had missed when shaving that morning. Jesus had insisted it was too late to drive him home. He was happy, he said, bedding down in the back of the car, telling Lindberg that he didn't trust motels as he had a cousin who worked up at the Paramount Pest Control Service on Riverside Drive near the Elysian Park Expansion who had had contracts to service motels across the city. "Vermin, lice, even in them upscale joints. I'm better here," he had said, patting the backseat of the Pontiac as if it were a first-class cabin on an Atlantic cruise liner.

That night on the badly sprung bed in the motel Lindberg dreamed of Adella as a couple quarreled noisily in the room next door. In his dream he was watching her from the bathroom of the Old Man's house again, as he had that first Christmas, but this time she turned as she reached the car and began to say something to him. But in the dream Lindberg couldn't hear the words or read her lips, and pressed his ear against the bathroom window in a desperate attempt to make them out. But there was nothing but silence when his ear was pressed up against the glass, and when he would turn to see if she were still there, he would see Adella leaning from the car, growing smaller as it pulled away, mouthing the same words over and over in an attempt to make him hear.

At 7 a.m. the next morning, Lindberg spoke to the Old Man from the phone in the motel lobby. It was close to the desk where the elderly receptionist, hair scraped back in a bun, had checked him in last night, scratching down the information from his driver's license into the motel's ledger. As Lindberg spoke on the telephone she would occasionally look up from her knitting and offer a vacant smile that showed her large teeth, yellowed at the gum line, her eyes magnified behind the thick round lenses of her spectacles.

"Those sick fucks." The Old Man's voice was dry and paper-thin.

Lindberg listened to his breathing amplified down the phone line.

"They sent a piece of her dress to the office."

"Was there a note?" Lindberg asked.

"No note." The Old Man paused. "Just a scrap of soiled fabric."

Lindberg felt himself retch. He swallowed it down, sour, hot and acidic.

"Well," Lindberg rallied, trying to hold back the panic in his voice, the rising sense that this was all beyond his control, that Jesus was leading him on a wild-goose chase. That Adella would never be found in this city with its two million inhabitants or that if she was, she would be like that girl in Gardena. Trying to hold back his anger at the Old Man for sending him instead of Chase. His growing fury and perplexity that any scheme, no matter how crooked or corrupt, that the Old Man was involved with might merit keeping the police at arm's length when his own daughter had been taken.

"I think we have a lead here," Lindberg said, steeling himself.

"Time's running out," the Old Man told Lindberg.

"Time's running out," the Old Man repeated, softer this time and with a sigh. Then he hung up the telephone.

In the motel parking lot Lindberg found Jesus sitting in the backseat of the Pontiac, hands across his lap. His apron folded in a neat square next to his sandwich box, stifling a yawn like a child who had arrived early to kindergarten.

"OK, now we go meet someone," Jesus said as Lindberg got into the car. He looked as if he had slept in his clothes, Jesus thought. Lindberg said nothing and started the engine.

"We are getting close," Jesus said leaning forward, patting Lindberg on the shoulder as a jockey at the Santa Anita racetrack might the flank of a horse he had just ridden in last across the finish line.

"Ricardo Eakins, but you can call me Red." Red was small and frail with a thin wheaten mustache. He wore an oversized satin Dodgers jacket. He looked like the kid Lindberg had once seen on the cover of a comic book in a drugstore. The three men sat down at a booth in the back of the diner on Olympic Boulevard.

"It ain't news. Crews been doing it for time immemorial." Red looked around the diner. A gray-faced couple three booths down were spooning puce-colored soup from their plates.

"Started with the Chinamen up in San Fran but they kept it in house so we never really got wind of it down here."

"Go on," Lindberg said, trying to sound patrician.

"They get to know a girl. Shoot her full of junk. Send a letter to Daddy demanding cash for her safe return."

"And?"

"And most times they get what they want. Plus it's low risk as the broad basically kidnaps herself."

"So the girl is involved?"

"Hard to say. Most probably she don't even know herself what's going on she's so full of dope."

He slowly patted himself down for a cigarette until Lindberg intervened and offered him one of his own.

"Thank you," he said nervously.

"So where do we find them?"

"Ah, that's the sixty-four-thousand-dollar question," Red sniggered.

"Our mutual friend didn't tell you?" he said to Jesus.

Lindberg turned to Jesus. Jesus shook his head.

"See, here's the thing, Pops, giving you an outline of this racket is a risk but a calculated one."

Lindberg watched Jesus's hands slowly balling into fists as Red spoke.

"You want to know where they're at, then I gotta ask around which means exposing myself, if you get my drift?"

"You want more money?"

"Got it in one."

"How much?"

"Well," he said, taking a long pull on his cigarette, "you have to ask yourself, Mr. Lindberg, sir, what's that little girl's life really worth?"

Red flinched as he finished his sentence as if half expecting some act of violence to be visited on him. But Jesus sat still and let Lindberg do the talking.

"I'll need to make a phone call."

"Be my guest."

Lindberg stood up and made his way to the phone booth at the back of the diner leaving Red and Jesus alone at the table.

"So what's the deal here, Sancho Panza?" Red asked, leaning back into the booth. Jesus said nothing.

"No disrespect, you don't strike me as the type to be caught up in this kind of caper. What angle are *you* working?" Jesus remained silent.

"You know what," Red said, lowering his voice, "together we could lead this guy a merry dance?" Red raised his eyebrows and leaned in across the table.

"Cover all our overheads for the year to come?" he said, rubbing two fingers together against his thumb. Jesus raised his index finger to his lips.

Red threw up his hands. "Have it your way."

They sat in silence until Lindberg returned.

"We can go up to two hundred dollars for information leading to the safe return of Miss Smart. Half up front, half when she's safely home."

"No dice," Red said instantly.

"I'm going to need," he paused, weighing up Lindberg, the wingtip oxfords, the gold lighter he had set on the table when he offered him a cigarette, the signet ring, the suit and the expensive fedora.

"Three, and all up front."

"OK," Lindberg said softly like a weary parent indulging his child.

At which Red, angered at being so easily out-negotiated, got to his feet.

"Give me two hours then meet me back here."

Jesus waited outside the diner while Lindberg walked the five blocks to the City National bank where earlier that morning the Old Man had told him funds would be made available should he need them. When Lindberg returned Jesus was leaning against the window of the diner wearing his apron like a short-order chef taking a breather from the kitchen, watching pedestrians stop to buy their papers at the row of vending machines outside.

"No sign of him?"

Jesus shook his head.

Lindberg slotted a quarter into a vending box and, lifting the hatch, pulled out a copy of that morning's edition of the *Los Angeles Times*. The plane crash he had heard about on the radio the previous day had been given several column inches on the front page. There was a grainy picture of the debris from the Lockheed Super Constellation taken from the cockpit of the plane that had been sent out to reconnoiter the wreckage.

Lindberg stood tutting to himself as he read the details of the tragedy; the names and ages of the victims listed in full, tourists, mainly, returning home to America. As Lindberg read the list of names, images of the dismembered bodies floating in the gray waters of the North Atlantic formed in his imagination. Then the images of the dead from the plane crash gave way to the dead girl behind the Dumpster in Gardena Chase had described around the Old Man's table. Only this time, in his mind's eye, Lindberg saw that the flesh on the girl's neck had been gnawed away leaving the white rings of cartilage on her windpipe exposed, and when he looked carefully the face he saw was Adella's. The image disappeared as soon as Lindberg snapped the paper in two, folding the article, with its list of dead Americans, closed in on itself. It began to rain, dark pools and rivulets forming on the asphalt. Jesus looked at his watch. Almost two hours had passed since Red left. The pair made their way back inside the diner. Lindberg stopped at the door and turning to Jesus said, "It's just so hard, you know, knowing she's out there somewhere." Jesus nodded, looking out at the office workers sheltering in the doorway of the building across the street.

"Somewhere out there," Lindberg continued, "I mean, she might just be right around that corner."

"We're close," Jesus said.

An hour later Red returned. He set the soaking sports pages of a newspaper down on the diner table.

The ink from the newsprint had bled on his hands. He wiped them on his pants. Lindberg pushed an envelope across the table to him.

"OK, for the record, Pops," Red said, sweeping a lock of wet hair back from his eyes, "there are no guarantees here. I put my head over the parapet and this is what I came back with. If it ain't right. then bite me. You and your boy here ain't getting none of this back. *Comprende?*"

Red slipped the envelope inside his jacket.

"Try this address." He slid a laundry ticket across the table. Lindberg turned it over. "Mention my name: there'll be hell to pay."

As Red stood up he unzipped his Dodgers jacket to reveal the hilt of a black pistol tucked in the waistband of his pants. He gave a saccharine smile and for a moment Lindberg was reminded of the freckled kid from the cornflakes commercial.

"And I'd move quick if I were you," Red said. "Word is, that girl of yours ain't long for this world."

The address Red gave them was a disused toy factory down by the 6th Street viaduct, where the shallow LA river sluiced across a wide concrete expanse, the air above criss-crossed with power lines. The rain had eased off now but the sky was still leaden, threatening a further downpour to come.

"This looks like the place," Lindberg said, the front wheel of the Pontiac brushing the curbstone as they pulled up. "So what do we do now?"

"Now we go and collect the girl," Jesus said in a matter-of-fact way as if taking receipt of groceries at his overstocked store.

A steep concrete walkway led up to the factory's entrance. The two men ascended the ramp, Lindberg gripping his fedora by the brim at his side, Jesus in his apron, carrying his aluminium sandwich tin. Lindberg wondered what a passer-by might have made of them—perhaps they would have seen a factory owner returning to the site of his bankrupt business accompanied by the foreman, who looked almost proud to be back at his former place of work, such was Jesus's manner as they ascended the ramp. There was a folding metal grille across the entrance and a large padlock, thickly caked with rust, hanging at the center. Jesus inspected the lock, weighing the brass shell in his hand, then from his sandwich box produced a pair of metallic-blue bolt cutters no more than six inches long.

As Jesus set to work cutting the shackle, Lindberg noticed for the first time the tremendous strength in his forearms, the ridged tendons flexing as he gripped the bolt cutters in his small hands. Lindberg watched the shackle warp, then the rusted body curl up toward Jesus. Then the broken lock fell to the floor. Jesus dragged apart the two halves of the metal grille. As he did this a noise made both men recoil. A pair of wings beat frantically at the air in front of them. A pigeon hung at eye level, the crown of its head thrown back, its claws splayed. The bird righted itself and flew out between the heads of the men. It was quickly followed by more birds from inside the factory. Lindberg ducked back as they flew out, squatting and shielding his face with his fedora. Jesus watched the birds ascend in a tight circle toward the viaduct.

"We kept a coop full of rollers when I was a kid," Jesus said as Lindberg rose to his full height and dusted himself down.

"One day me and my big brother got in a fight over which birds was mine and which was his. Ten years old, I come home and find him slashing their throats with a box cutter. His friends standing around the yard howling and laughing as them birds tried to take off. Blood all over the concrete and these rollers that I'd raised from chicks just flapping, trying real hard to make it up into the air. A few of them got over to the other side of the street. I remember them in the bottom branches of the trees there, dripping blood down onto the sidewalk, then one by one just falling out with a thump." Jesus shook his head. When the birds had disappeared from view Jesus went back to his sandwich box and took out a Cordahide flashlight.

"Come on," he said. "Let's go get her."

The windows at the back of the factory had been boarded up. The ground floor was stripped of most of its machinery, only a few wooden work benches remained. At the center of the factory floor the beam of the flashlight picked out a trestle table turned on its side. A scrawny pigeon with ragged tail feathers and a glossy boil on one of its pink feet cooed and pecked at the concrete as it strutted in a circle around the table. A row of rotting, mildewed cardboard boxes stamped with Chinese lettering were piled three high the length of the far wall. With the flashlight Jesus picked out the remains of toys from the production line that someone had sorted into uneven piles: water-damaged patchwork rag dolls, grimy plastic baby arms, the chassis of tin cars. In the far corner there were signs of a bonfire: a pile of pale ash in a circle of broken bricks. Jesus walked over and placed the palm of his hand over the ashes. He rose slowly to his feet and turned the beam of his flashlight in a ninety-degree arc along the ground. The beam froze a few yards from the spent fire on what looked like dried coils of human feces covered with newspaper.

"Hobos," Jesus said. "These ain't our guys."

He swung his flashlight up to signal that the men should continue their search for Adella on the floors above. As they looked up they saw that from the ceiling someone had strung wires full of baby-dolls' heads: bald, red lipped, the eyes rolled back into their plastic skulls. The stairs were barricaded by two upturned shopping carts, their frames bent and dented. They looked as if they had been fished out of the river. The carts had been placed on top of each other and stuffed with rags and old newspapers. Concrete breeze blocks buttressed their base and a pair of scaffolding poles were set in a diagonal cross behind them. Behind the scaffolding poles a soiled mattress had been leaned on its side. When Jesus peered in, shining the flashlight at the steps beyond, they glittered with broken glass that had been scattered across them.

"So maybe we take the elevator."

Jesus led them back across the factory floor to the service elevator. As he thumbed the faded red button there was a rumble from the basement. Slowly the cable in the elevator shaft began to move and when it appeared, Jesus opened the cage for Lindberg. Inside the elevator it stank of ammonium and the sharp tang of stale beer. Lindberg entered with his handkerchief pressed to his face.

The first two floors the men examined were empty. On the first one the wooden floorboards had rotted and Jesus had turned and caught Lindberg by the elbow when his foot had passed straight through one. The third floor was almost identical to the one below: the same flaking paint and exposed wires, the same rusted vents and hastily emptied storage cabinets, the same gauges and switches and broken brown bottles of chemicals that had been left behind when the factory was abandoned. There was still no sign of Adella, no sign of human life at all. But from here they were able to access the stairs again. When they opened the fire door onto the fourth floor the windows were no longer boarded but were broken into pinnacles of jagged glass. It took the men a moment to adjust to the light.

"Hear that?" Jesus said, placing a finger at his ear and cocking his head. Lindberg nodded as they listened to the broken, staccato notes drifting down from the floor above them.

The men moved slowly along the stairs that led down from the fourth floor. Lindberg following Jesus as he softly picked up and put down each foot, careful to avoid standing at the center of each stair lest any sound betray their presence in the factory. As they reached the final flight Jesus pressed his body against the wall and moved slowly, his small frame hunched tense as he crept toward the door. As he watched him Lindberg was given an intimation of the man who had taken the blockhouse at Iwo Jima. With the back of his hand, Jesus opened the door a fraction and looked through. A beam of light was cast sharply against the wall of the stairwell. Through the gap Lindberg could make out the corridor. It was carpeted and in good repair. He assumed that this floor must have originally held the administrative portion of the factory. At the end of the corridor the men saw a figure leaning against a doorway.

"What now?" Lindberg whispered to Jesus.

"You go ask for her," he replied. "I'll take care of the rest."

The man looked like a middleweight. He had a thick neck and his dirty blond hair was greased back in curls from a deeply lined forehead. His nose was hammered flat like a piece of misshapen modeling clay. He was dressed in a powder-blue suit, arms folded. Beyond him at the far end of the corridor Lindberg's eye was drawn to a door that opened out onto a fire escape. Lindberg reasoned this must have been the entrance through which, if Red was right, Adella had been led. Lindberg wondered if they had had to drag her through the door, if she had put up a fight, kicking and screaming as she was bundled up the staircase, or if they led her slowly, her mind blurred from the dope they had hooked her on in the months leading up to her being snatched from her bedroom in the Old Man's place in the desert. The two scenarios competed for prominence in Lindberg's imagination: Adella screaming like a frightened infant, then Adella silent as a widow walking in a funeral cortege as they led her into the room. Lindberg wondered if the men he had seen her get into the car with that Christmas as he watched her from the bathroom might be the men they found behind the door guarded by the middleweight in the powder-blue suit.

"We're here to collect Miss Smart," Lindberg said.

Before the man could respond, Jesus exploded toward him, his fists suddenly around the man's lapels. As Jesus pinned him against the wall, the man's head flew back like a dummy in a crash test. Lindberg heard his teeth smash together as Jesus slammed the man, who stood a foot or more taller, over and over against the brick wall. Lindberg saw the man's eyes glaze over, oily, opaque almost. Then just when Lindberg thought Jesus was going to kill him, he stopped and lowered him to the floor, gentle now, with the practiced calm of a hospital orderly putting a patient in a chair. Jesus brought his face close to the man.

"So now you going to tell us where she is, *claro*?"

"Yes," the man said, blinking rapidly as if he was staring up at the sun. Lindberg saw dark blood oozing out from the man's nostrils and one of his ears. Lindberg had stood with his hands in his pockets throughout the frenzied attack. When he brought his hands out, he saw the white half-moons he had dug into the flesh of his palms. Standing over the dazed middleweight Jesus looked down and raised a finger to his lips. The middleweight nodded as Jesus then ran his finger across his throat in warning. In the inside pocket of the middle-weight's powder-blue jacket Jesus found a service revolver; inspecting the weapon he saw printed on the plate on its handle: Property of the Los Angeles Police Department. He showed Lindberg.

"He's a cop?" Lindberg asked.

"Nah, these things get lost or stole. Maybe he killed a cop. Or maybe he just bought it off of some-one who did."

Jesus cocked the pistol and opened the door.

The squalid room was bathed in red light. The men saw that the music they had heard earlier had been coming from a single player: a man in his fifties sitting on top of a tea crate holding an oboe. His lips were chapped and he kept licking them, then playing broken phrases on the instru-ment. There were several other men in the room who had seemed oblivious to the commotion Jesus had caused outside. There were mattresses on the floor and by the mattresses leather straps and several glass syringes stamped Excelsior. Lindberg saw the floor was strewn with yellow tubes whose red lettering told the reader they contained: Soluble Hypodermic Tablets of Morphine Sulphate that had been manufactured by the Fraser Tablet company in New York. Adella lay on a divan by the window in the far corner of the room. Her track-marked arm hanging limp, a little patch of white foam gathered at the corner of her mouth. Her lipstick was smudged and clownish. Lindberg pointed her out and Jesus walked toward her.

"Adella? Adella? *Habla me, chica.*"

Jesus pressed his fingers to her wrist. He began to pat her pale face roughly. Lindberg looked at the men in the room; half a dozen frozen in his gaze as if at gunpoint. The man with the oboe clutched the instrument to his chest. Others slowly buttoned up their shirts, or simply rolled over away from the action on their dirty mattresses. No one seemed willing or able to take responsibility for Adella.

"Who brought the girl here?" Lindberg asked. There was silence.

In the corner of the room, slumped against a large green filing cabinet, Lindberg noticed a man rocking slightly. His knees were pulled tight up against his chest, his chin pointing down hid his face and showed only a thinning crown of hair. There was an expensive-looking jacket nearby that Lindberg suspected the man of throwing off as he heard them enter. Lindberg turned to Jesus who nodded having also noticed the man. Lindberg helped Adella up from the divan, her thin arm hanging over his shoulder.

"You take her down to the car now," Jesus said, setting down his sandwich box and inspecting the room in the manner a decorator might having been called in to price a job. Lindberg lifted Adella; her body seemed to weigh almost nothing as he made for the fire escape. He turned at the doorway to see Jesus wiping his hands on his apron, then pulling down the tattered sheets of fabric that had been pinned at the windows. The men squinted as light poured into the room. Jesus walked to the door they had entered through and held it open for Lindberg. Lindberg heard the lock click closed when he was out in the corridor.

As he carried Adella down the fire escape, Lindberg tried not to listen to the noises coming from inside the room. As they neared the street below Lindberg heard the sound of the police service revolver discharging once, twice, then after a brief pause, for a third time, after which there was silence.

When Jesus returned to the parked Pontiac, Lindberg saw that his apron was flecked with blood. His right hand had ballooned and was bruised with four purple welts across the knuckles. It reminded Lindberg of an injury he had once seen sitting ringside with Angelica's father at Madison Square Garden on the hand of a bantamweight who had gone a vicious twelve rounds against an opponent who had been carried from the ring on a stretcher. Lindberg had watched as the boxer's trainer took off his gloves and cut away the bandages to reveal the hand beneath. He watched as Jesus took off his apron and folded it across his bruised knuckles.

"Tell Mr. Smart I have a name for him if he want to pursue this any further." Lindberg nodded.

"This is for you," Lindberg said, handing Jesus an envelope containing cash he had withdrawn earlier at the City National. Jesus placed the envelope inside his aluminium sandwich box.

"*Claro*," he said, sounding tired. "Now we go back to Rambla Pacifico."

Jesus had set up a camp bed in the back of the store. It was dark out and the room was lit by a kerosene lamp. Lindberg watched Jesus spooning a thin broth into Adella's lips. He thought of his own girls up in Maine and the spring they both came down with chickenpox and he had nursed them through their fever. Something in Jesus's manner reminded him of how he had behaved when his daughters woke up mumbling and terrified from their fever dreams.

"She needs to sleep a while," Jesus had told him. "Then maybe you take her home."

It was close to dawn the next day when Adella finally woke. Jesus and Lindberg had spent the evening and the night taking turns to watch at her bedside. The Old Man had insisted Lindberg keep her there until she was well enough to be driven back. He had given Lindberg the number of a private nurse and a doctor he trusted in the Pacific Palisades should she require medical attention. He had forbidden Lindberg to take her to a hospital.

"No. You just watch over her," the Old Man had told him. Already he could sense the Old Man's concern now turning to anger. Anger that he was sure in part would be directed toward Adella. He wondered what Chase had been saying to the Old Man in his absence, what seeds of doubt he had been planting in the Old Man's mind, who he might have inculpated in the story. He even wondered if Chase might try and paint him as somehow complicit in Adella's disappearance.

"You know he always did like her," he imagined Chase saying to the Old Man, his face blurred by the smoke from one of his cigars.

That night Lindberg had stood in the back of the store smoking a cigarette, replaying the events of the past twenty-four hours. Jesus, who had busied himself carrying out inventory by flashlight as Adella slept, came and joined him outside. It felt to Lindberg like the two men had spent months together and he wondered if Jesus had misunderstood Cooper's statement on the beach. It was strange seeing Jesus back in the store and stranger still that the store seemed more of a hobby than a going concern. As if Jesus collected the tins and cans inside on its cramped shelves as some men did the rolling stock and cast-iron figures on model railway sets.

As the men stood in the yard, Jesus busy with a long-handled broom, Lindberg had asked him what kept him here. Remarking to Jesus that this seemed an out-of-the-way spot for a convenience store.

"I like it," Jesus said, bending down and scooping up a handful of dry soil from the yard. He let the ribbon of dirt run away through his fingers.

"In a month the big rains come and wake up the valley. Nights you hear the owls swooping in to catch the mice."

"I guess so."

"After the wildfires last year, they try and buy me out. Want to build some fancy houses here. But I say no. I like it just fine. I'm not selling."

"Everybody has their price."

Jesus frowned and shook his head.

"I'm going nowhere."

A little after dawn Lindberg decided it was time to get back on the road. He wanted to leave with the light while it was still cool enough to drive. Adella's fever had dropped but Lindberg feared the effects of the sun and the drive back to the Old Man's house. Jesus helped him carry her out to the Pontiac.

"Thank you," Adella whispered to Jesus as he positioned her across the backseat of the car. It was the first she had spoken since the men found her at the disused toy factory. Jesus nodded but said nothing and turned and walked back to the store, with no more thought than when helping any customer load up their car. Lindberg felt suddenly fatigued and too tired himself for any formal good-bye. "Let's get you home," he said and started the engine.

As he pulled away he saw Jesus standing in the doorway of the store, lacing a fresh apron below his breastbone. He signaled for Lindberg to wind down his window and walked over to the car, resting a hand on the rubber lip where the glass sank into the door, looking away down the track as he spoke.

"Ever need help again, maybe you give me a call."

"Sure," said Lindberg, "I'll do that."

Jesus banged the roof with the flat of his hand. Adella asleep in the back wrapped in the Army surplus blanket did not stir. Clouds of dust, bright in the first light, rose up around the automobile as Lindberg pulled off down the red dirt track. Back to Rambla Pacifico and other roads that would lead him through the early morning to the Old Man and that half-built hotel somewhere out in the desert.

# Wave-Riding Giants

McCauley watched as the boy's father carried him the last two hundred yards out to the ocean. He was a tall child, or should have been, but his legs had wasted away and were floppy and white and in their translucence made him think of two wilted sticks of spargel. For a minute he watched as the boy's father held him there, cradling him in the breakers, the surf from the Pacific foaming up around him, as if the force of all that water might do something for those ruined limbs. McCauley hadn't been out to the beach or the boardwalk the recreation room overlooked since he fractured his pelvis last year. A girl in her teens on a skateboard pulled by two toy terriers had knocked him down at the corner of Paloma Avenue. He heard the hiss of her acrylic wheels on the concrete, and had a sense of something approaching at speed. He was turning when she had collided with him, her shoulder slamming against his ribs, sending him falling awkwardly backward. It was a closed fracture under a dark plum bruise that curled around from his hip to the top of his buttocks. But there was limited bleeding, the doctors told him, and the butterfly-shaped group of bones had stayed in place.

In the past he enjoyed walking among the crowds on the boardwalk as the evening came on. The tourists and their families, the groups of sunburned bums and drifters on the concrete benches with their out-of-tune guitars, the Latino kids with their muscular Staffs and Pits outside the tattoo parlors, hot in their dark jeans; it had been a salve to the welling loneliness in the years since Dolores died. And although there was a notice in the recreation room advising all residents to remain in the building after dark, he liked the boardwalk best just as the light was fading.

Instead he now had a pair of binoculars heavy as a candlepin bowling ball, like the ones they had used on the convoys, except that this pair had *Kriegsmarine* stamped on them. One of the caregivers, Vanessa, plump under her white nurse's shift, got them for him from an antique show up at Big Bear Lake where her boyfriend, Carlos, had taken her one weekend last April. To tourists walking past on the boardwalk, McCauley must have seemed a benign, spectral figure behind the window six feet above them. He would offer a wave if a child riding on their father's shoulders caught sight of him. In the Senior Housing Facility where he lived for the past eight years, there was a cold-cuts buffet each Wednesday, uniform slices of ice-cream-pink meat marbled with white fat laid out on trestle tables, and tepid melon Jell-O every Friday. In the recreation room, where he spent most of his time, there was a small library donated to by the daughter of a former resident who owned a surplus bookstore in Santa Fe. It included a set of books by Zane Grey that McCauley liked: *The Vanishing American*, *30,000 on the Hoof*, *Riders of the Purple Sage*, *The Light of Western Stars*. Once a month a handsome Dominican man named Conrad, who was prematurely gray and played keyboard at the Shul on the Beach, came to give a little concert inside the lime-green walls of the recreation room. He enjoyed hearing Conrad play, his concentrated, beatific smile, his neat, even features and shining complexion. Despite these distractions the binoculars Vanessa had bought for him were the most significant source of pleasure. There was usually something to hold his interest on the expanse of sand across the boardwalk: the yellow Coast Guard truck cruising between the breakwater lifeguard stations or the yachts on their day races up along the coast. But lately when he had come to take the binoculars out of their case, they had begun to remind him of the convoys he served on in the war. Those hours in the fire room, the rocking hull, the smell of the hot lube and combustion fumes coming through the vent shafts. Memories he hadn't thought on for decades seemed to cling around the binoculars.

He had signed on at the Lower East Side recruiting station in the new year 1942. He queued in a foot of snow on January 2, after seeing the first posters go up in the window of a barber's shop in the Bowery: "Man the Guns—Join the Navy," a picture of a tanned sailor stripped to his waist breech-loading a three-foot shell into a deck gun. "Remember December 7th," "Navy Needs Young Patriotic Americans." He had seen there and then the chance to turn himself into a citizen with motive, purpose, and direction like the son of that mother whose testimonial ran in the promotional literature. There was something right about the words. They were words he would like to associate his life with. After he was sworn in, his parents three rows from the front in the audience, he was sent by rail to the Naval Training Center near Geneva in the Finger Lakes of New York State. There, identifying an aptitude, they trained him to work and maintain the ventilation systems: the change rates; the ducts and pressure drops; all the repetitive, necessary work to keep a ship afloat. It was bitterly cold in the Finger Lakes but nothing could have prepared him for the cold on the boat as they did circles of the Arctic, protecting the convoys delivering food to Stalin's Russia. Setting out from Iceland, under Svalbard and, after a fortnight at sea in summer, dropping down into Archangel. It amused him sometimes to think that he was helping run supplies back to the continent his grandparents fled from.

At sea working in the engine room he would often think about his mother's mother, Baba Spevek, with her low, pendulous breasts and skin that smelled of sweetened dough, telling him about the winters back in Minsk when she was a girl. About how she and her friends, Alena and Aksana, who had an ulcer on the cornea of her right eye that had left it milky and purblind, whose mother let her stay home from school for weeks on end, once snapped the penis off a hog that had frozen solid. His grandmother would sit in the tea room she owned, and where McCauley's mother sometimes left him when she went off to work when his father was away, a boy with a Scottish name in a world full of Russian women, telling him how they chased one another around cobbled winter streets holding the thin, sparkling wand of the dead hog's wiener, icicles gathered on its corkscrew glands. He was glad they got away when they did. Baba Spevek's brother had worked building the sets at the opera in Minsk and his sons had worked there too before the war. He found out after the war in Europe was over that they were all killed, half-starved, just blocks away in a labor camp on Shirokaya Street, the empty opera house piled full of all the things that the Nazis had stolen from them: paintings and pocket watches and whatever else they could get their hands on. He remembered Baba sobbing when the letter arrived from a niece of hers who had survived because, she said, a Nazi soldier had pulled her out of a car on account of her blue eyes and blonde hair. He remembered the letter she sent to Baba, with its strange Cyrillic script. It was the only time he ever saw Baba cry or receive a letter. He was en route to the Pacific but never made it as "Little Boy" and the *Enola Gay* got there first. His ship had dropped anchor at Long Beach and was given twenty-four-hours' shore leave. He remembered thinking to himself as he walked out into the sunlight and the sight of the cranes and all the industry of the port with the other ranks that this was where he was going to make his home. That with an American Craftsman cottage, like the ones he'd seen written about in the newspaper, and with a piece of land, a man could start to build a whole world for himself out here.

After demobilization he decided he would stay in Los Angeles. His first thought was to try and find work in construction but with the GIs just back from the war the market was crowded at the bottom. Lines of men waiting on the street corners every morning just to see if they could get a day's work picking fruit out in the valley. Before the war had come along and given his life some shape, he had worked a couple of summers helping fix up theater sets on Broadway. His mother's cousin was a seamstress at the Astor and so she got him the work. Painting and cutting out backdrops mainly, filling in the silhouettes of the parts of the city he'd never been to. They were long days for low pay but when the curtain went up on the first night there was no feeling like it.

He was sleeping on a mattress on the floor of a furloughed engineer called O'Sullivan in Brentwood and eating breakfast and dinner out of cans when he first got to Los Angeles. He remembered how after they won the war in the Pacific all along the coast it was like a carnival. The bonfires on the beaches, fireworks being let off, quarts of liquor and sickly sweet rum punch being drunk. It was another world. How could he have lived twenty-three years and missed this? He remembered how they were terrified out on the West Coast all through the war that they were going to get bombed to rubble. When Chester Nimitz was out at Midway fighting off Yamamoto's armada, John Ford made a movie that had them all feeling like it was going on right there in their backyard. He couldn't say for certain what he was doing those first months in Los Angeles. Drinking too much, he was sure. He remembered several fumbled trysts on beaches at night, and mornings waking up next to women in trailers or backseats of cars, the windows thick with condensation. All in all, he thought, he was just trying to put those years at sea behind him. Working on forgetting. It seemed there was so much to forget back then.

McCauley's ship rammed a U-boat once, south of Jan Mayen Island on the return leg of his convoy's winter route. The signalman spotted the conning tower out in a squall. They had fired off star shells but the rain got in the way and they lost sight of her. A few minutes later she was spotted again and they trained the 4-inch and the pom-pom onto her, and after three depth charges were dropped the U-boat surfaced and that was when they rammed her. He remembered the sound of metal on metal, the deep thud reverberating through the bow of the ship. How after the U-boat keeled over all the guys were out on deck hollering and wailing as if Joe DiMaggio had just hit one out of the park. How they then let her have a few belts of Hotchkiss, for good measure, which is when she rolled and sank down into the sea, stern first. The rain had turned to snow and some of the U-boat's crew started to surface in the beam of the searchlight. Their faces bloated and waxy, they looked, McCauley thought, like mannequins from a department store window.

In 1945 there was a union bust-up and all the workers at the studios went out on strike. Eight months they were out on the pickets and McCauley was offered some hours over at Metro working as a carpenter on the sets. McCauley wasn't in a position to turn it down. He had been getting into quarrels over nothing in particular and had spent a night in the cells due to a brawl with some infantrymen from Texas after drinking with O'Sullivan at a bar in Redondo Beach. He could feel his life starting to run away from him, never sober long enough to make a good decision. When he first started at Metro, he was still living on O'Sullivan's floor but after four months working every hour of overtime Metro offered and once or twice moonlighting on other sets, he put down a deposit on a Craftsman in Venice. He took pride in his new home, especially the garden. Thirty feet by twelve with a southerly aspect, he began growing lupins and mariposa lilies, and he even planted two palms out front. The house had sat empty all through the war. The day McCauley moved in, he found a paper lantern at the back of the closet in the kitchen. Next to it there was a tiny drum with a symbol inked onto the skin and two black beads threaded on string so that when the handle was twisted from side to side it made a noise. He figured the place must have belonged to one of the families Roosevelt had sent out to the desert when the war in the east began.

It was not long after McCauley moved into the house in Venice that Adra Fishkin, a man he knew growing up in the Bowery, arrived on his doorstep. Fishkin's family were from Minsk too. Fishkin had always been a sickly child, rubella then scarlet fever in quick succession before the age of ten. Once when they were young, playing on the street he fell and cut open his leg on a broken beer bottle outside one of the flophouses where you could get a bed for twenty cents. McCauley had taken him back to the rooms his mother shared with her cousin and her family a few blocks away and watched as she boiled a piece of silk thread and sewed up the gash in his leg right there and then on the sofa. Fishkin's father had ruined his lungs on his way to America. He lived in a room above and sometimes McCauley would see him standing, jaundiced, at the top of the staircase. Fishkin had seen some terrible things with MacArthur out east on the islands where the Japanese wouldn't give up. He even looked different now, thinner, his shoulders hunched when he walked. More like his father than the boy McCauley remembered from the Bowery.

Fishkin was en route to New Mexico. Some of the guys from his unit planned on starting a bail-bond business in Alamogordo, and they had promised him a fifth of the company if he could stump up some capital. Fishkin, or Fisher as he had started calling himself, ended up staying with him for the best part of three months; there was always some-thing delaying his leaving, a check that was yet to clear or some issue with the application for a license for the bail-bond business down in Alamogordo. In truth, McCauley remembered, it was nice to have a face from back home out there in California. And when he'd answered the door to him that Saturday afternoon two days after Ascension Day and seen him standing there in his demobilizing suit, his protective instinct from those days in the Bowery had kicked in. The guys he worked with at the studio had all been together before the war, more or less, and he guessed the newbies only reminded them of the ones who didn't make it back.

Most evenings when McCauley finished up at Metro, he and Fishkin would sit on the porch, on the two rocking chairs he had found in the yard and fixed the spindles on, playing hands of poker and telling each other stories from the war. Fishkin had a collection of Army-issue V-Discs with Leonard Feather's All Stars playing numbers that they both liked and these recordings became the soundtrack to their evenings on the porch. Sometimes when they had both drunk enough Kentucky Tavern, they would start to quarrel, throwing down the cards onto the tea chest they played on top of, bickering like an old married couple grown sour in each other's company. Once McCauley remembered nursing a split lip for a week after they tumbled down the porch steps when Fishkin had taken a swing at him. Few of McCauley's stories compared to the ones Fishkin told him those nights out on the porch when the liquor had loosened him up enough to talk freely. Even now he carried images from those conversations with Fishkin: the bodies his patrol had come across with their skin burned off and impaled on top of bamboo poles, so badly charred they couldn't say for sure which side they belonged to. It had taken Fishkin longer to tell McCauley how he had taken a shovel to the skulls of the wounded Japanese infantrymen as they lay prostrate on the ground. It was the sound that stuck with him, the blunt thud of the spade on the backs of their skulls, their flattened black hair. The last story Fishkin told McCauley was a few nights before he left for New Mexico. It was about the time an infantryman in his unit had run his bayonet into the guts of their young sergeant who had lost his mind and whose scream-ing threatened to give away their position. Another soldier had cradled the sergeant, holding a soiled handkerchief to his mouth, the handkerchief turn-ing a deep crimson as the boy bled out. A horsefly trapped inside the house, batting against the window as Fishkin told the story of the young sergeant and how they had all sworn an oath there and then to tell no one if they ever made it out. Some nights after they had played all the hands they could and drunk all they needed to drink and each gone off to their own bed, he remembered Fishkin screaming himself awake in the room next door as some image from the jungle came rushing back to him.

One Saturday afternoon a month or so after Fishkin arrived, McCauley took him out to the boardwalk with half a mind on heading up to the Santa Monica

Pier where Spade Cooley and his band were putting on a new show, when they saw two girls talking by an ice-cream stand. Fishkin despite his troubles always had a way with the ladies. He once got a date with Betty Rowland, "the Ball of Fire," after they watched her dance burlesque in West Hollywood a few years before she was convicted of lewd conduct. On the boardwalk that afternoon Fishkin had gone strolling over to the two girls and shouted "Attention!" as if he were a drill sergeant and they were standing on the parade ground. McCauley remembered thinking that he had gone too far. But these girls thought it the funniest thing on God's earth, and were laughing out loud, which only encouraged Fishkin, who started marching around them, shouting obscenities. The girls were off to Corona Del Mar to meet some friends who were surfing there. A man was giving an acrobatics display on a hobbyhorse a few yards away as they talked, so it was hard to keep their attention focused on him and Fishkin. Eventually they asked them if they wanted to tag along. McCauley remembered Dolores had on a cotton summer dress with roses with green stems appliquéd on it that had faded in the sun. Lips painted red and her hair all pinned up at the back, a few fine strands fallen loose and the breeze moving them around her neck. A pair of silver SolarX sunglasses. Even now sitting in the recreation room he could summon up that first image of

Dolores at will. On their first date McCauley took her up to the track at Santa Anita. She ate a grilled filet mignon steak sandwich as if a morsel hadn't touched her mouth in days. He had turkey with cranberry sauce and shoestring potatoes. They made love that evening quickly, urgently, in the backseat of his car parked in an alleyway three blocks from her parents' house in Westmont. The same dress she wore that afternoon on the boardwalk hitched up around her waist. Her bare legs fuller, stronger, more muscular than he expected. He remembered how Dolores laughed out loud when he asked if he was her first.

*The Green Room*, that was a phrase McCauley associated from those first days with Dolores. That's what they called it when you were inside the barrel of a wave. Dolores's friend Patricia was crazy for the guys who did the wave riding. The week he met Dolores on the boardwalk, Patricia had been a runner-up in the competition for Queen of Newport Beach at their Tournament of Lights and before the war she had been one of Earl Carroll's dancing girls. Her first boyfriend drowned up at Pillar Point Harbor and by all accounts Patricia had been a little unhinged ever since. A real wild woman double feature, Fishkin had christened them after that first day.

After Dolores and McCauley got together at weekends, they would drive his Oldsmobile to Malibu to watch Patricia's friends surfing. Sometimes they would hitch a trailer on the back and spend the night up there. That's how McCauley came to make a board for Bud Morrisey. They were sitting around on the beach one evening by a big fire McCauley had spent the afternoon setting while the guys were out in the water, and he and Bud got talking. McCauley explained that he was in the carpentry business, working over at Metro. Bud told him about this hand-built hollow-wood board he wanted made. "White cedar," McCauley told him, "that's what you'll need." And when Bud asked if McCauley could do it, he told him it would be an honor. He had watched him out there on the south swells and thought the man was an artist. He had passed a whole afternoon admiring him on a long board coming in on those ankle-high wind-swell waves. He spent weeks on the board for Bud Morrisey, working on it in the evenings after he finished up at Metro, feathered piles of blond shavings growing slowly in the garden. The first few frustrating evenings he was caught up in making the stands and the blocks, screwing the angle brackets into the patio at the back with a masonry bit, but they wouldn't take so when that didn't work he ended up filling a five-gallon bucket with sand, which got the job done and just about held the stands in place.

McCauley remembered on that last day looking at the finished board, not wanting to let the
thing go, thinking how beautifully the grain ran the
length of the waxed wood and pleased at how good
the redwood inlay with Bud's initials looked. The
whole board weighed no more than twenty pounds.
McCauley wished he could take it out. But he had
never learned to swim. He remembered driving over
to Bud's place with the back windows wound down to
accommodate the length. And how he only charged
him for the wood. They kept in touch and McCauley
gave him a lathe when he set up his own wood shop
making boards down in Redondo Beach. A few years
ago on Memorial Day McCauley got talking to a kid
with a fiberglass board on the boardwalk. The boy
was there with his wetsuit rolled down around his
waist and his board, with its colored graphics sten-
ciled on, tucked under one arm. McCauley asked
him about Joe Quigg, Buzzy Trent, Gard Chapin,
Moe Charr, Bob Simmons with the withered arm.
But he had never heard of any of those guys and
just stared at him and shook his head. They were real
giants, McCauley remembered telling the boy.

McCauley often thought about those classic
summers up in Malibu, with Dolores and Patricia
and whichever of the boys she was dating at the time.
Fishkin tried his luck with Patricia before he left.
He had taken her to see *Breakfast in Hollywood* with

Bonita Granville. McCauley loaned him a suit and his second-best tie, with a red and white zigzag running down the front. He remembered Fishkin standing on his porch, and being on his knees with a mouth full of pins pulling in the suit pants so they fitted at the waist. Fishkin got nowhere with Patricia but McCauley heard from Dolores that he promised to send her a postcard every week until she agreed to a second date. The cards kept coming for a couple of years, with misspelled, enigmatic messages and postmarks from all across the United States, then one day they just stopped and no one ever heard from him again. The night skies in Malibu seemed to go on forever and like no night sky McCauley had ever seen, not even up there in the Arctic. McCauley remembered being out on the beach, Dolores and Patricia busying themselves flipping over sides of skirt steak and fat sausages. The guys all teasing him for only going into the ocean up to his ankles. McCauley saw it like this: that some people followed baseball but that he followed these guys. He was a fan and unashamed of it too. It wasn't just the sport those guys knew how to live. They seemed to him to glow out there on the ocean. McCauley often thought back to how when he was there with them the war seemed like another lifetime. As if the boredom and bodies and burned faces in the water all belonged to someone else. When Dolores got sick, eight years ago and three months after they moved into the Senior Housing together, it was stories from those classic summers he would tell her.

They had only moved on account of the location and were among the youngest couples in the building. It was a choice they had made together having never had children and because of the rate that was available to McCauley as a member of the Alliance of Theatrical Stage Employees, a membership he had kept up even after he stopped working for the studios and had taken a job teaching woodworking at a community college in his sixties. It just all seemed to make such sense and they both wanted to be back near the ocean. They convinced themselves it would be more like a holiday resort than a retirement home. He still remembered Dolores was so excited to be around young people again down there on the boardwalk. McCauley would sit and tell her stories about those first summers they spent together as they filled her up with chemicals to beat the tumor that was eating at her bones. A tumor they first spotted as a plum-sized lump on the side of her elbow. Dolores had gone on to work as PA to the company's director at the fabricated metal products firm in Long Beach. He was the son of the man she had begun working for in '46 and they had always done well by her, including a good health insurance package when the company was bought out by a Taiwanese conglomerate two years before she retired. The stories of those summers up in Malibu were the only thing that made her smile toward the end.

There was only one story that neither of them ever mentioned. On an afternoon in the early summer of 1949, McCauley got home from Metro. The lead in the picture he was working on had fallen ill and this had led to a contractual wrangle between her lawyer and the studio, which in turn had meant closing down the set early that day as both parties attempted to negotiate a compromise. He experienced a pleasant lift as he drove home from the studio, a few hours stolen back from his working day. As he parked outside the house in Venice he noticed that the front door was open. There was music drifting out of the porch and onto the pathway. As he got to the gate he could see Patricia in her underwear asleep in the living room with the ceiling fan slowly beating at the air above her. McCauley remembered how he was laughing when he saw Patricia and thinking that he had missed one hell of an afternoon. Then as he looked farther into the house he saw Moe Charr, with his shirt off, and his cousin who they'd met a couple of weeks ago up at Malibu—both large, hand-some men who between them could have formed half of a decent set of linebackers on a football team. Then he saw Dolores dancing sandwiched between them in the kitchen. He watched the three of them moving slowly across the tiles that he'd laid himself a few months ago. As McCauley walked up the pathway that led up to the house, he saw Dolores drop to her knees, and then lost sight of her behind the kitchen counter. He saw Moe leaning back, spreading his large hands across the kitchen counter. Then Moe's cousin running his hand through Dolores's hair. McCauley saw the cousin's hand tightly at her jaw, the way you might fit a muzzle on to a greyhound. The next thing McCauley saw was Dolores's hand gripping at the counter. This came into focus as he walked up the path. McCauley remembered how Moe's head was tipped back now and how his Adam's apple was bobbing up and down as he swallowed hard. And as quickly as it had happened, Dolores up and laughing and then both men taking her by the wrists and pulling her into the bedroom at the front of the house. McCauley froze outside, halfway along the path and through window screens looked on for what might have been seconds or hours at the blurred shapes the three of them made. Obscured behind the screens and farther through the drawn lace curtains.

McCauley did not know what had happened in the bedroom. He walked into the living room and shook Patricia awake, saying her name as loud as he could manage. He stood and watched her come around noticing something childlike, innocent almost, about the way she roused herself from her drunken sleep. It was several minutes before Dolores came through. She had on her dress now. She wrapped her arms around McCauley and kissed him on the cheek. A few seconds later Moe came through buttoning up his shirt, rubbing his eyes. He let it be known, looking at Patricia but addressing McCauley, that he'd been sleeping it off in the den. He shook McCauley's hand and patted him on the back and asked him if he knew his cousin? Pointing his thumb at the large man with bloodshot eyes who stood behind him. McCauley told him he did and then Moe Charr poured McCauley a tumbler from the Seagram's Gin, one of two they had got through over the course of the afternoon, saying to him, "Tough day, huh?" Then the two men sat there talking in the living room for a few minutes before Moe and his cousin said they better be on their way. Patricia asked them if she could get a ride. That evening Dolores was teary. She crouched on the sofa crying. Then stayed up crying in the hallway all night. The next morning McCauley found her slumped by the wicker table where they kept the telephone, the nightdress he had put out for her pulled across her like a sheet. For days afterward she didn't talk. McCauley had to phone in sick for her for three days in a row. Then one morning she snapped out of it and continued with their life as if nothing had happened. Not long after, Moe went off to Waikiki for the surf and never came back, but they ran into his cousin once on the forecourt of a gas station.

McCauley wanted to talk to Dolores about that afternoon when she was up at Sinai. The things he hadn't asked her had pressed on him. He remembered her lifting up her hand from the hospital bed and putting two fingers at his lips. Telling him to hush now. She had beautiful hands, McCauley remembered, soft and small, the cuticles and half-moons always perfectly neat. McCauley guessed there were other stories she wanted to talk about more while she still had time to listen. And anyway, he was decades late with his questions. In her final month McCauley visited Dolores on the female-only ward at Sinai every day. In her last week he moved her into a private room. Then the time came when he couldn't stand to see her suffering any more. Couldn't stand the daily drive up there to see the frail, unlovely thing she had become, the machines doing her breathing for her. Her cheeks sunken and her skin yellowed like a smoker's fingers, its elasticity all lost. Standing there in those last days looking at Dolores, McCauley felt stupid. It was an error that they never had children, that there was no pretty, patient daughter taking time from her own busy life and family to help soothe her mother as she died. An error that they hadn't tried again after her first miscarriage in 1949. How the sight of her bleeding in a bathroom stall in Reno where they had gone to get their relationship back on track had shaken them both. And now there he was, an old man with no family, no sons or daughters, just a sick wife being kept alive by wires and drips.

It was clear to McCauley what he needed to do, what he should have done weeks earlier when the pain was at its height, not now when Dolores was just a husk of herself, slipping in and out of consciousness. The curtains in her room were drawn already as McCauley kissed Dolores on her forehead, softly as if her skull were made of paper, the slightest pressure might damage it.

He remembered how he walked over to the wall and turned off the switches on the machines she was connected to. One by one the small red and green lights went out on the gray plastic monitor. McCauley waited ten minutes sitting on the folding chair by her bedside, holding Dolores's hand, which was cold to touch, then he walked back to the wall and flicked the switches on and pulled the red plastic triangle which hung at the end of the alarm cord. In those moments waiting for the nurse to arrive and take her pulse, and tell him Dolores had passed and offer him her condolences, it was that summer afternoon in '49 with Moe Charr and his cousin that McCauley thought about. He thought of Patricia asleep on the sofa, a dark nipple half-exposed from her brassiere. Moe, the big, handsome, powerful man he was, who McCauley had admired so much out there on the waves in Malibu, their stilted conversation over two fingers of warm gin, and how he wouldn't look him in the eye as he left but shook his hand and encouraged his cousin to do the same.

# Black Bear in the Snow

"Black bear in the snow, tra-la la-la-la," Randall sang as he lifted the baby up and over the plastic bars of the crib. He ran his fingers lightly over the indent at the back of the infant's skull where the bone plates had yet to fuse. Randall knew there was a name for this, something elegant sounding. A word that made him think of sunlit squares in Paris when he first heard the midwife use it. "Black bear in the snow," he sang again softly, the words fuzzy and half-formed as he paced with the baby across the laminate flooring, stepping through the patches of light that fell from signs on the strip mall that overlooked the apartment.

"Brown girl in the ring!" Thelma would have corrected testily had she been at home. But Thelma was at Gunnerson's Restaurant, working a late shift. After a late shift she always came home angry, the eczema blooming raw on her inner arms. It was an anger Randall could never defuse, not now and not when they had met as awkward freshmen in their

first semester at college in Minnesota. Randall's
father had refused to speak to him for a week when
he told him this was where he intended to study
and not at the seminary, as had been his mother's
dying wish. Whenever Thelma got home from a late
shift, Randall would be up at his computer, the TV
muted and glowing in the corner of the apartment.
Setting her keys down with a sigh, she would pull the
night's tips from her apron pocket. Randall would sit
typing lines of code onto the green screen, trying to
avoid her gaze, the towering processor and external
hard drives piled up around him, like a child inside
a makeshift fort. Thelma would look up from the
crumpled dollars on the Formica counter to Randall
and then back again. But Thelma wouldn't be home
for an hour yet. Randall was alone with Joey (Joey,
not Joseph, as his own father had been). As he sang
he remembered the drive he had taken to Alberta
with his father, the spring his mother went into the
hospital. How his mother's sisters, Frances and Annie,
had arrived on the Greyhound bus from the soupy
warmth of Fulton County to the chill of that Illinois
spring. His aunts, with their battered brown suitcases
each fastened with a piece of frayed elastic, standing
in the hallway of the house his father would default
on that coming winter. Frances tutting as she looked
around the entrance hall, Annie running a finger
across the dust on the sideboard, imagining how their

younger sister lived with this salesman she had met at a dance when she was seventeen.

Soon after his aunts arrived, Randall remembered his father saying they were going to take a trip. "How about it, sport? Just you and me, two guys gone a-huntin'." He had pinched Randall's cheek, and the stinging flesh seemed to signal his entry into the world of men. Aunt Annie had bought him a hat to wear, red-and-black check with ear flaps that folded down and fastened under the chin. Randall remembered moving through the bright silence of the boreal forest, the late snow creaking as he stepped inside his father's boot prints. Stamping his own tightly laced boots through the thawing muskeg. The frost lingering on the iron-colored pools of water as he and his father moved toward the hide. Walking into the forest between the boughs of the blue spruces that looked like they need only to be hung with lights to be fit for a front room at Christmastime. Behind them, deeper into the woods, the mottled trunks of firs and poplars rising up from the shadowy dark, melting snow dripping from their branches. The forest seemed to fold the light in on itself. His father consulted his map and took a pull from his hip flask. Then with a backward glance and a wink, "C'mon kid, almost there."

When they had reached their destination, they pulled away the trimmed pine stems that covered the mouth of the hide. They had hunkered down in the smell of wet soil and stale piss that Lambrey, who his father served with in the Marines and now ran the lodge, had led his father to the day before. Randall's father rested his binoculars on the slot of the hide, a low plywood pillbox someone had painted green last summer and strewn with leaves and netting. Five hours they sat there, his father nursing his rifle in the crook of his arm, without a hint of movement from the spot where Lambrey had promised a bear was sure to appear. And this despite the money Randall's father had given him to bait the mouth of the cave. No bear ever emerged.

Randall remembered the long walk back to the lodge at dusk. The flurries of birdsong from the wild canaries and warblers that seemed to follow them out of the forest, back to where they'd parked the truck, through the bare and budding branches as they walked with their heads down. That night, in the bar of the lodge, Randall watched his father drinking beer after beer, unable to slake his thirst. The same four songs playing on the jukebox, the mechanical arm raising and lowering the disks as Randall sipped a watery Pepsi. He remembered the web of veins in his father's reddened eyes, the tubular, pale pastel threads on the edges of his bulbous nose. "We always wanted a sister for you, Randy. A little girl. But now . . ." His father shrugged, then looked away, working his tongue into the corner of his mouth as if trying to dislodge a piece of meat stuck between his back teeth.

Later, when he was older, Randall remembered asking what had happened to his mother. His father, bloated, unrecognizable now as the large athletic man who had taken him hunting, reclining in the La–Z-Boy in the state-funded nursing home in Peoria, said, "They cut out her womb but the cancer came back," as he flicked between a game show and a black and white movie where Frankenstein's monster stood by a lake with a little girl who held out a bunch of flowers to him.

Now Randall's own son, Joey, was fourteen years old. His chin and mouth blistering with acne. Randall always thought the angry, hot pustules must have made it agony to smile. It was thirteen years since he held him in their apartment above the strip mall on Lincoln Boulevard, eighteen since he and Thelma had dropped out of school, Randall convinced there was a fortune to be made in computers; certain, to the point of obsession, that the people at the Palo Alto Research Center—to whom he had written letter after letter—would find a place for him on their team. Randall still remembered the feeling of nausea in the exam room as he flunked the entry test for the organiza-tion. His mind a perfect blank, unable to reformat even a few simple lines of code. The long walk back across the parking lot and home to the apartment that he'd been living in with Thelma ever since they found out she was going to have a baby.

There followed a decade of watching his boy grow in monthly increments. Driving up from San Diego, where he worked as a technician in the computer labs at a Christian high school. The first weekend of each calendar month taking Route 5 along the coast, through Solana Beach and Encinitas, past the Marine Corps Base Camp at Pendleton, which never failed to trigger a memory of his own father, duffel bag slung across his shoulder, back from Saigon, a hero in their neighborhood, having served as an eighteen-year-old in the war in the Pacific in 1945 and then volunteered for Vietnam, walking to greet him across their square of lawn.

Randall would arrive at the house in Beverly Hills where Thelma had made a home with a lawyer, fifteen years her senior, who she had met, of all places, at Gunnerson's and who, she screamed at Randall one night, "treats me like a real fucking human being." That was the night their arguing had grown so loud the building's manager, an Armenian who Randall had played checkers with only a week ago, called the police. When Randall answered the door, one of the officers had seen Thelma over his shoulder weeping like a fallen woman in a silent film. He had stared at Randall and, without looking in beyond to Thelma, asked, "You OK, ma'am?" his knuckles whitening around the handle of his nightstick.

On his monthly visits Randall would always park his beige station wagon a street or two away from Thelma's house, walking through the neighborhood as any other tax-paying resident might. He would often imagine things had played out differently, that he was returning home after a week away in Europe or China, from speaking at a conference on some software he had designed that looked set to revolutionize the tech industry, or some new form of supply chain management for decentralized manufacturing, the applause of conference delegates still ringing in his ears.

Today as Randall walked the winding path to the door of Thelma's house, past the patches of well-tended jonquils and violets, the big jacaranda blooming on the corner of the street, he watched a hummingbird alight on a cylinder of red nectar that hung in the doorway, taking sips from the sugared water. He set his thumb on the doorbell, the porcelain button cool in its brass surround. A few moments later the maid answered, a plastic laundry basket under one arm. She ushered Randall into the palms and soft arches of the bright hallway and went to fetch Joey.

In the five years Randall had been coming to the house, he had never strayed farther than the hallway. Occasionally in the wintertime the maid, whose name he still did not know, would bring him a cup of eggnog—or a fruit cup if it was summer. Here, as he waited for Joey, he was given only hints of the life his boy might lead in the days away from him: the photographs inside their silver frames that over time had grown to cover the top leaf of the black baby grand. Holiday photographs; the family laughing in the sunshine of a Hawaiian beach or crammed onto a gondola by the butter-colored walls of a Venetian canal, their shapes reflected in the muddy water; Thelma and the lawyer and Joey and their two girls with their sickly, bean-curd complexions and lengths of ribbon tied in their hair.

Joey came down, wiping the sleep from his eyes with the sleeve of his sweatshirt. He offered his hand for his father to shake. Randall hated this. A country club affectation, that Cody, the lawyer, had foisted onto his boy. The attempts to dislodge Randall from his son's life had lessened over the years. "We need a clean break," he remembered Thelma telling him as he called from a phone booth, at a time when he thought things might still be mended.

Randall was now tolerated, filed away by Thelma and Cody somewhere between the maid and the graduate student from UCLA who came to tutor math; a low-end domestic who could be relied upon to entertain their difficult eldest child for a few hours each month. Impersonal, distant, to be occasionally thanked and thought of no more. Randall was convinced he once saw Thelma unthinkingly make for her checkbook when he returned Joey one afternoon.

"Joey," Randall said, as they stood in the hallway that morning, "I have a proposal I would like to put to you."

"OK," Joey shrugged, his eyes cast down under his long fringe.

"I would like to take you hunting."

"OK," Joey said, as if his father's statement had been inevitable.

"My father took me hunting once and, well . . ."

Joey looked down at his sneakers. Randall paused. He had come across a magazine about hunting, the pages loose from their staples inside the shiny cover, as he waited in a dentist's reception room last month. As he read about the recent developments in bow hunting and hunting with dogs, it brought back the frustration and excitement of that trip to Alberta with his father. A numinous set of feelings that on recollection he didn't know whether to laugh or cry at. It must have shown as the receptionist, a Thai girl with her dark hair in French braids, leaned across the counter to offer him a waxed-paper cone of water.

"It'll make a man of you," Randall said, trying to find a voice big enough to fill the statement. He had rehearsed his speech in the car on the way over, addressing himself in the rearview. What had he expected from Joey? A blunt refusal? A direct appeal to his mother, bellowing up the wrought-iron and marble staircase for her to come down and "tell this asshole I don't have to go?" Some sign of life from his teenage son? But instead Joey just nodded at his sneakers.

Randall came back a fortnight later to collect Joey. He had had to ask permission from Thelma and Cody to take his boy away for the week. Randall sent an e-mail to them, laboring over the tone of the request in the computer labs after the school closed. Then came a wait of five days, in which Randall imagined the conversations Thelma and Cody must be having, before the reply: SURE. LIAISE WITH KATIA (CC'D). THELMA. Katia, Cody's secretary, let slip that Thelma and Cody planned to take a week in Colorado to celebrate their anniversary and this at least solved one of their child care problems.

It was agreed that after a three-day drive to Alberta and three days at the lodge, Randall would put Joey on a plane back to Los Angeles from Calgary. Randall had been tightly bound by the divorce proceedings: his move to San Diego cited as "abandonment," the small amount of hash he had once been cautioned for possessing (he had gone out to buy it at Thelma's request so heavy had her period been that month) an indicator of some larger, more sinister addiction. "Gateway drug," he remembered Thelma's attorney, a balding man in a double-breasted suit, who smelled of expensive peppery cologne, solemnly intoning to the judge.

Randall was feeling hopeful the morning, two weeks later, when he collected Joey to begin their trip. The drive up had been sunnier than he expected and he had stopped and drunk a beer at a place by the ocean watching a group of windsurfers in wet suits struggle with their sails as an instructor bellowed directions at them from the sand. When he arrived at the house Joey was waiting with his bag by the curb.

"I've made some tapes," Randall said, leaning across to open the glove box. "Stuff you might remember. From when you were little."

Joey picked up the cassette box.

"They *still* make these?" he said, working his thumb into the case. Randall smiled.

That first day they drove through Las Vegas, where Joey had never been. Adding a few hours on to their journey to move slowly down the main drag past the hotels and casinos, Las Vegas tawdry and underpopulated in the early afternoon light.

"Somethin', ain't it?" Randall said, craning his neck and resting his chin on the top of the steering wheel the better to see the reproduction Eiffel Tower above the dry tops of the palm trees in the central reservation.

"Mom and Cody think gambling is wrong."

"Well, everything in moderation, I guess." Randall was relieved to hear the lawyer referred to by his first name and not as "Dad" as Joey had sometimes slipped and called him in the past.

"Yeah, Cody represented a billionaire who was suing a casino for some bet they reneged on."

"Did he?" Randall replied flatly, then lightening his tone, "You ever gamble?"

"We play poker at school sometimes after class."

"Oh yeah?" said Randall. "Ever win much?"

"Nah, just quarters."

Randall smiled.

"Some guys from class play online. But, you know, that's pretty dumb."

A little before midnight they arrived at their motel in Spanish Fork, just south of Salt Lake City. After they dropped their bags in the room—small and hot and smelling still of the previous occupants— they walked a hundred yards across the parking lot and ate a taco at a Mexican Ranchito that was closing for the evening. The lights were out in all the booths except theirs and a waiter in a stained tuxedo pushed a mop from a bucket of gray water around the floor. Back at the motel Randall took the foldaway and lay awake listening to Joey's breathing, watching his boy's chest rise and fall, his lips parted slightly, the circuitry of veins on his eyelids flickering as he dreamed.

The next day they broke their journey just short of the border with Canada. Turning off State Highway 464 to a Motor Inn that served tourists arriving at Babb Airport. The Motor Inn was owned and run by the Blackfeet Nation, the tribe that had historically occupied the plains between here and Alberta. As they approached, they saw the peaks of the Glacier National Park in the distance. It was still light when they arrived and they sat on the hood of Randall's station wagon in the forecourt. They watched a light aircraft descend to the airstrip. Its wings first dipping left, then right, like the arms of a man on a high wire trying very hard not to fall.

"Wouldn't you just love to get up in one of those things?" Randall asked.

"Yeah, I guess," Joey replied. Then, after a pause, "Must be a little dangerous."

"That's what they train you for. They don't let just anyone take the controls." Randall stopped himself as he found his enthusiasm for the subject overrunning his knowledge of it.

As Randall checked in, Joey flicked through a brochure produced by the Blackfeet Nation in the lobby of the Motor Inn. Joey was smirking. On the page he had opened there was a photograph of a man in a suit with a diamond-patterned tie and an unfashionably large pair of glasses. The man might have passed for a partner at Cody's firm, someone Joey was used to shaking hands with at corporate picnics and days out, if it wasn't for the feather headdress he wore. Its long eagle feathers painted red above the brightly beaded trim. Randall noticed the receptionist looking at his smirking son. He turned and frowned at Joey then immediately regretted it. He saw his boy tense up, all the small doors and passages, the ways of communication that two days on the road had opened up, slammed shut. Joey tossed the magazine on to the table. "I'll go get the bags," he said. Joey refused to speak to Randall for the rest of the evening. He went straight to their room, where he lay on the bed in his sneakers, sending messages to friends back in Los Angeles, snickering at their replies, occasionally looking up and scowling at Randall.

The following morning Joey was still resolute in his silence. He sat with his headphones on in the passenger seat, playing muffled death metal loud enough for Randall to hear. They stopped for gas and Randall came back to the car with a sandwich and a can of soda for Joey. He looked at it blankly then took it, and in acknowledgment left off his headphones for the rest of the day.

The lodge Randall stayed at with his father had closed down, but online he had found a place an hour away. The first morning was spent on target practice and safety instructions, where Randall had lied nervously about his experience as a huntsman, which extended no further than the single trip with his father. Once Joey got over the sound and the force of the rifle's recoil he had proved a good shot, first hitting the outer rings of the target and then a large wooden cutout of an elk fifty yards out on the makeshift range.

"You done this before?" asked the instructor, Kennet, a bearded man with pitted skin in a camouflage baseball cap, whose office was adorned with photographs of himself, his arms draped around the necks of huge dead moose and bears.

"Nah, it just takes concentration," Joey had told Kennet as Randall looked on.

The training had concluded with the issue of luminous orange vests and Kennet distractedly flicking through a book with black and white diagrams of bears and other animals showing their organs and advising where to aim for a clean kill. Randall had declined the offer of a guide but spoke privately to Kennet about the best hides and spots to head for the next day. Places they were likely to make a kill.

The next day Randall tried to keep their spirits up as they walked through the woods. The good weather on the road had given way to rain and then to snow the farther north they drove. It was raining now. The rain turned the snow to a slush colour of wet ashes.

"Well, this is us," Randall said when they reached the hide Kennet had marked for him on the map a mile or so from the main trail through the woods, "all's we have to do now is wait."

Joey threw down his backpack, then flung himself on top of it. The trees dripped clear water from their branches. The finches and the warblers sang. Father and son took turns to keep lookout. At one point an elk froze before them on its thin legs. They watched it stay perfectly still, then suddenly break into the woods. Afterward Randall dozed for half an hour. Nothing much was said between them, the occasional "You OK?" from Randall and the occasional "Yeah" from Joey. Around midday Joey quietly unwrapped their picnic. Last night in the store at the lodge, Joey, unknown to Randall, had bought two energy drinks, a bag of potato chips, a foot-long sandwich to share and a box of plums. Joey unpacked the food with care and great seriousness, placing each item on a hand towel from the bathroom of the motel near Babb Airport.

"What?" Joey asked when he caught Randall looking at him.

"We're going to need food, right?"

"Right."

As the afternoon passed, the rain eased off, the weak sun slowly wheeled around above the woods. Their drowsiness after eating offset by the tension of waiting for the bear to appear. "We're not going to see one," Joey told Randall repeatedly over the course of the afternoon. "Let's wait and see," Randall said, though he was far from convinced and with every hour that passed felt a mounting tension. When the bear finally appeared, it was smaller than either of them had expected: a young cub of a hundred pounds, the size of a sheep or large dog. It caused Joey, at the opening of the hide, peering down the rifle's sight, to freeze.

"There, Joey, there," Randall hissed, stabbing the air with his forefinger, "pull it, shoot, shoot."

Randall saw Joey's hand tremble, then his thumb take off the safety catch, his body hunched tightly over the rifle that now seemed much bigger than the boy who was holding it.

The sound of the rifle discharging caused the birds to scatter from the branches, their wings beating like a round of halfhearted applause, a dusting of snow falling to the ground. The animal let out a low yawning mewl, then collapsed on its side, crashing through a pile of brittle wood above the snow line. The clear air was hung with sulphur. Joey looked down at the bullet casing on the floor of the hide. A few yards away the animal lay dying in the snow, its body crumpled from the impact of the bullet that entered cleanly through the chest cavity behind the front shoulder. Randall took a step toward Joey, putting his arms around his son. He listened to the sobs as he pressed his face into the folds of his anorak. "You did good, son, real good," he said, stroking the back of Joey's head. Things would be all right now, Randall knew it.

# The Burning Ground

Alannah would always come at two o'clock as she had on her first visit. But they never talked about how they might exist outside of the confines of the studio. Then at Easter a fortnight passed without her visiting. He had delayed his own trip to see his sister in Harrogate. By the third week, when two o'clock came he was pacing the studio, snapping the slats in the battered brushed-metal blind, peering down onto the parked cars on the street below. He had first met Alannah and her husband at the same party. He had dismissed the husband: a tall man, in his thirties, in a striped shirt and red braces, whose boyish good looks had begun to slacken. He was explaining to an acquaintance the difference between a bull and a bear market. There was a touch of French or Swiss to his accent, which seemed an affectation. He might have dismissed the man's young wife too: timid, pale, unexceptional, had a mutual friend not shepherded them together and on to the common ground of his former tutor at the Slade. She seemed impressed that there was anyone alive who could still remember him, let alone who had been taught by the great man.

After their first meeting he did not think again of Alannah until the friend who had introduced them phoned to ask if she could pass on his details. She explained about the monograph Alannah was working on and how he might lend some important insights. He agreed but that first afternoon her visit slipped his mind. The sound of the buzzer jolted him from his work. There followed a difficult conversation over the intercom as he failed to recognize her name wrapped in the little loop of static and feedback. Only once she was standing in his studio did he recognize her from the party and recalled the arrangement made via e-mail a few days earlier in the Internet café where twice a week he went to pick up his messages. As they talked he noticed how her skin reddened in uneven patches on her neck and across her décolletage and the hard, level confidence of her stare, a poise he had not noticed at the party.

Three weeks after Easter when eventually Alannah arrived, she was forty minutes later than usual. There was a pause as she stood before him in the doorway. He wondered if she had second thoughts. If time away with her husband reminded her of the fullness of her life and the extravagance of her time with him: the painter whose reputation had been in decline for two decades now. He imagined her in her car, parked a few streets away, her hand hesitating on the key in the ignition. Standing there before him she seemed smaller, tanned, changed by her time abroad: carrying the mood of the French town whose name was printed on the calico bag that held her tape recorder. The tape recorder she had continued to bring with her to his studio as evidence, if an alibi were needed for her husband. He stood for a moment registering the ways she had changed since he last saw her: a new leather bracelet, her hair now parted at the side with a tortoiseshell comb, a little more makeup than she usually wore.

They did not speak. He set about reclaiming her, first lifting off her jacket, then digging his nails in hard below her shoulder blades, pressing through the fine linen of her camisole as they kissed. Pushing her against the crossbar of a racing bicycle that had sat unused in the entrance way for the best part of a decade. Her teeth clashed against his dry lips, drawing blood. He tasted it ferrous and metallic at the corner of her mouth as they kissed.

They made love at first on the camp bed and then on a patchwork quilt laid on the cold linoleum floor, an old horse blanket by their feet. Gripping at the curves of her hip bones as the gas heater burned on nearby. Looking down at his own body; slackened with age into folds of formless skin, its

contours of tightly packed wrinkles and pucker-
ing. The sounds of a London afternoon outside,
schoolchildren shouting excitedly as they waited
for the bus and the sound of the fast train passing
on the bridge. Afterward, he traced the outline of
her bathing suit across the soft flesh of her lower
back before she rolled away from him and sat up,
pulling the quilt over her knees. She was tense after
they had made love, as if she had arrived intending
not to, running her forefinger and thumb through
her hair, rapidly working from strand to strand;
searching out a single hair coarser than the others,
she would then lift it gently from her scalp, twisting
it between her fingertip and the pad of her thumb.
He had learned from Alannah that in her teens she
had been in the habit of pulling out her hair. A
*trichotillomaniac*, she had said, carefully enunciating
the word, making the term seem almost comic. At
the clinic her parents sent her to for treatment she
learned about the associated, much rarer, condition
*trichophagia*, what they called Rapunzel syndrome,
where sufferers would pull out their hair and swal-
low it, causing, over time, the tail of a hairball to
reach down from the stomach into the intestines.
She told him how the image had been enough to
arrest her own relatively mild condition. Though
the habit of searching out the coarser hairs still
remained in times of anxiety. He watched her kick

the quilt from her legs then walk, without speaking, to the windowless shower room at the back of the studio.

When occasionally they did meet in the world—at gallery openings and once at a party for a mutual friend who was recovering from breast cancer—Alannah was warm and cordial and calm; indistinguishable from how she might greet any other senior artist she had worked with or interviewed. He accepted he had no right to claim her, hoping in time her visits would increase, that she might begin to feel the necessity of their intimacy. Knowing that if he challenged her, or invited this, she might disappear from his life altogether. There had been other women over the years of course. Married and unmarried, some younger, some older. The married made fewer demands or rather different demands, demands he found easier to fulfill. He had been married himself once, in his twenties, the year after he left the Slade. It hadn't lasted and they had lost touch. She had died. He came across the obituary by chance in *The Times*. It seemed to him surreal, to think that thirty years ago they had lived together, shared a bed, made a home as best they knew how. Her daughter, who was eager to learn more about her mother's early life, came to visit him at his studio a few months after she died. She had her mother's features but was much taller than the woman he had married. But after thirty years without contact, the dead woman in *The Times* was a stranger with whom he had shared a brief part of his remote past. He had been attracted to her daughter and sensed an attraction on her part to him.

Remembering his afternoons in his studio with Alannah, there were certain images he would return to; faint rain pooling in the grooves of the corrugated-plastic skylight, the radio at the foot of the camp bed, the barely audible voices, Alannah's clothes in an untidy pile. In darker moods he wondered how many other studios she had visited with her tape recorder stowed in her bag, if every artist she had interviewed was afforded the same treatment. That everything that followed her climaxing—those short tight breaths she drew in through her front teeth as she came—was make-believe or self-deception. He looked for proofs from the past as a holy man might rake through the entrails of some dead animal.

The final night around her table in Tufnell Park, he had studied Alannah, trying to absorb what was most elemental about her. He sensed the dinner had been engineered as both a farewell and a rebuke. That Alannah had needed to show herself next to her husband, to prove she was resuming the role of the faithful wife. Each time her husband asked a question on the economics of his profession, he had referred him to his gallerist, Delaney, who sat two places down, knowing full well his last show of unfashionable still lifes—found objects accrued in his studio over the years; seashells from the beach an hour's drive from his sister's house, obsolete electronics picked up at the flea market in Deptford, begun as exercises with no coherent theme—had sold poorly to Delaney's regular buyers.

He would turn and continue his conversation with the woman to his right, an Australian literary agent with a mass of very dry straw-colored hair, keeping Alannah in view across the table. Watching as she laughed at her husband's jokes or laid her hand on his shoulder. He wondered if it had been a gamble for her inviting him, a final thrill wrung from the dying affair. Or if in their year of afternoons together she had grown to know him well enough to make an appeal to his better nature this evening. If she had seen through his gruffness and reluctance to commit to coming when she had phoned to invite him and knew he would try to please her, that the night would contain no dramatic declarations for the guests to discuss in the back of their minicabs home.

He acknowledged how easily he had allowed himself to submit to her willed civility. And later, he would reflect that being there was itself a kind of pleading, an appeal for her to take him back. For her to return to him as she had on those afternoons throughout the year: uninvited, unannounced and wholly welcome.

In the summer months he had learned to recognize the sound of her car coming to a halt on the street outside, the light metallic clunk of the driver's side door of her Citroën. He would grow expectant as she made her way up the concrete steps of the dilapidated former garment factory that housed his studio and several others, wiping his hands on the sides of his jeans, swilling a glass of tap water around his mouth to wash away the taste of unfiltered cigarettes and strong tea, growing tense before she pressed the buzzer. It was in the summer that she bought him the brushes. Handed to him three days before his sixty-fifth birthday, in a velvet-lined box tied with a red bow. She explained, solemnly, that she had bought them with money of her own, from an advance she had received for a short book based on her monograph, that she would start to write over the summer.

It was five years now since he learned of the twin boys Alannah had had with her husband. Overheard, in fact, at a crowded party to mark the end of an art fair. An overweight American woman in a silk caftan and Lycra leggings, proclaiming to a man in a blazer, that Alannah's newborn boys were "darlings, just darlings." His back to the conversation, he had felt himself flush, his face burning from the bridge of his nose to under his eyes. Standing in the noisy, forensically bright room he had seen it all: her swollen body transformed and unrecognizable as the one he had held; Alannah lying on the bed in the maternity ward; her husband working loose his cuff links as he paced the corridor, a cigar in cellophane in his breast pocket; the gray-green faces of the wailing infants in the midwife's hands. He had phoned her at home shortly afterward, something he had never done before, and when her husband answered had been at a loss as to what to say. The two men listening intently to each other breathing down the line, in rooms a few postal districts apart, neither saying a word until eventually he broke the silence and asked with a curtness he could not disguise "Is Alannah there?" The husband gave a little snort—he took perhaps to be derision—then called back, "Sweetheart, it's for you" and then more softly, "Here, let me, I'll do that." By the time Alannah was at the phone and asking, "Hello?" her voice rich and weary and freighted with a mellifluence that comes only in the aftermath of some unalloyed happiness, the same rich, weary new voice that must have been fielding calls from well-wishers over the past weeks, he had simply hung up, his mouth half-set in a stiff grimace, holding the plastic handset firmly and for a long time against the switch hook as if drowning something unwanted in a pail of water.

Now all that remained were the brushes. In the first year after they were given to him, they had painted Saudi heiresses in their overheated Knightsbridge apartments, the air outside as he walked from the tube, sweetened with the smell of confectionery pumped out from Harrods. They had painted Gold Cup-winning horses in their stables, filmed by rows of security cameras at the Surrey homes of their breeders. He would drive down with Delaney to jobs always framed as favors for friends, who were admirers of his work, with some money to cover his expenses. Both men knew the situation was unsatisfactory. It was Delaney who suggested the residency in California. He phoned him at the studio one morning to tell him of another artist of his who had just returned and how he was fairly sure he could secure a place for him, if he was interested: "I'm sixty-five, Delaney," he had told him. "Think of it as escaping England for the winter," Delaney replied. "It'll add decades on to your life. I promise you." He had laughed and told Delaney he would think about it.

A winter in Los Angeles turned into a year. The Foundation treated him with a respect and reverence he found difficult at first but then relaxed into enjoying. When at the end of the year they approached him about a fellowship, tenured with the Foundation for a further five years, he accepted. A lawyer had argued that his client, as a painter of portraits, specifically in oils, possessed a specialism the state required. In the way Delaney had back in London, the Foundation would suggest contacts who were interested in sitting for him and would be happy to pay, wives of show runners and retired producers. He had watched a sitter in Los Angeles recommend him to a friend on her cell phone as he sketched her barefoot under a camellia japonica at the far end of her garden where they had gone to catch the end of the light.

For the first year in Los Angeles the novelty of elsewhere had underwritten him. Through the Foundation he had met a broader, more sympathetic group of people than he had expected in the city he had come to in order to forget. Life in the impossible village, as he once heard it referred to by a photographer friend in a phrase pulled from the journals of Edward Weston, had proved tolerable. The photographer told him with relish how Weston had detested the place, this city of uplifters lacking what he found in smallpox and poverty in Mexico. How he had encouraged all sensitive, self-respecting people to leave. But he had not left. Slowly the place had made its claims on him. The light, the absence of clear seasons, the cloud that sat low along the coast in May and June, and occasional days of rain only endeared the city to him. Each gave his life a welcome sense of stasis. The Foundation that had covered the cost of living had arranged a show at a small gallery in West Hollywood at the end of his first year there. When tired of the city he would drive out to the desert, following the Southern Pacific freight cars past the wind turbines at the neck of the Coachella Valley.

Now he would spend his working week in Los Angeles traveling between the bungalow he rented in Venice—the powder-blue paint flaking from its paneled exterior, the Indian laurel shedding leaves on the uneven flagstones outside—and his studio downtown, both provided on a peppercorn rent from the Foundation. Occasionally he would visit the houses of his sitters out along the Pacific Coast Highway in the Palisades or up in Malibu. And every evening after using them, the brushes that had been Alannah's gift were painstakingly cleaned in the sink next to his oversized tumble dryer then laid out along the yellow shelf in the front room he used for painting. On taking the bungalow, the first thing he did was remove the screens from the windows and savagely prune the crape myrtle and the camphor overhanging from his neighbor's garden.

The winter he had moved to Los Angeles his first drawings had been of the carousel in the Hippodrome on Santa Monica Pier. He would sit inside the airy wooden building, watching young families come and go. Drawing each of the forty-six horses, with their weird snarls and contorted mouths, occasionally catching glimpses of his face in the mirrored panels as the carousel turned; thinner than he had been in London. Fixated by the rise and fall of the horses in the two inner rows and the otherworldly music from the Wurlitzer. He walked to the Hippodrome at four o'clock each afternoon, then as the low light was at its dying best, would position himself outside, sketching the bright heart of the carousel as it spun at the center of the now near-empty wooden room. Once at the Hippodrome he had watched a wedding party arrive. The two maids of honor riding side saddle in their lavender silk dresses, the groom and his best man whooping and boisterous as the carousel spun. The bride had worn a cream gown with elaborate folds of lacework down the front and a pair of pearl earrings on thin silver chains. Her smile had reminded him so completely of Alannah that he had grimaced as she looked out at him from the carousel. He must have seemed an odd sight, the tall old man, thinned down, with the contorted face on the folding stool in the corner of the Hippodrome.

With a second show at the small gallery in West Hollywood planned and a number of studies of the carousel sold, he found he was no longer drawn to images he knew would please Alannah. When working at the studio, a bright room on the seventh floor of a disused bank, he began to walk the streets nearby. On Olive and Margot and Catesby he found himself fascinated by the faces of down-and-outs. He became obsessed with the details of decay that they wore about their bodies. His first painting in the studio had been of the teeth of a man whose face had been ravaged by years of methamphetamine. He had worked from a Polaroid he had taken as the man leaned up against a whitewashed wall by a Dumpster in a parking lot on Margot Street. He painted details from the man's face in close-up, so at first the viewer saw only the pink of the gum line, the caramels of his cashew-shaped teeth and the wide red hairs of the mustache. Next came a series of studies from the white-ringed staph abscesses on the calf of an intravenous user he photographed on a mattress outside the Grand Prix Auto Body shop on Olive Avenue. The abscesses, blown up large, were unrecognizable until their context was revealed later in the series.

In that year with Alannah visiting his studio in London he had worked from memory on studies of her—stooped naked at the sink or squatting as she showered in that windowless bathroom at the back of the studio. Images that were all, he later realized, of her preparing to enter the world and return to her husband. Images of her stripping herself of any traces he may have left. Now downtown he spent more and more time talking with the men who congregated in the streets in the Wholesale District. Reprising his London habit of sleeping in his studio, sometimes he would go down early in the morning and stand by their bright nylon tents pitched in front of the closed shutters of the pet stores and fabric shops. He would give them a few dollars in return for the Polaroids he took. Downtown he felt a new hunger growing for the details from the lives of the homeless: their nails, their soiled clothes, the littered groundsheets of their tents. Men he might have been indistinguishable from if photographed.

Four years since leaving London, five since hearing of the birth of Alannah's boys, six now since that last afternoon in his studio. Life had taken on a superficial stability. A couple of messages a month on his answering machine meant he was never short of work, and once his reputation had been established he was free within reason to name his price, charging several thousand dollars for a commission. When occasional e-mails would arrive from his sister's daughter voicing her concern for their mother's deteriorating health, a recent fall or blood test, even this news seemed to be softened by his distance from it. It was a world as other and unreal as the world he had made on those afternoons with Alannah in his studio.

As a student he had had a severe allergic reaction to penicillin his GP had prescribed for a chest infection at the end of his first term. Once the forty-eight-hour fever had passed, his body had been covered in a raised webbing of lipstick red. It wasn't until late in the next year that it had really begun to fade. It had taken years more for it to disappear completely, appearing again faintly if he ran or got too hot. In a vague way now he remembered this rash when he thought of Alannah and those years she had always been in the background of his thoughts, as his new life continued around him: exhibitions, dinners, dates with divorced women a decade younger than him, drawn to his minor celebrity in certain circles, who sensed a hollowness at his core they could not account for and he was unwilling to explain.

After the ink-wash drawings of the horse heads on the carousel, and the acrylics of the homeless men downtown that he exhibited in his second show in West Hollywood had sold, the brushes still remained. Daily routine had smoothed the rough edges of his life. Five days each week at his studio downtown. Every second weekend spent working on a commission— lately at the home of a senior accountant at Time Warner who lived on the Bird Streets. An exhibition at the gallery in West Hollywood now promised every eighteen months. Waking with the light in his Venice bungalow. His midmorning drive downtown along the Santa Monica Freeway in his big, comfortable, air-conditioned American car. His regular lunch in the cantina on Grand Avenue watching Mexican game shows on the ancient television mounted on the wall. A bottle of Pacifico some evenings at the café on Venice boardwalk, that stunk year round of candle wax and old incense, where he would chat with the waitresses. Over time these novelties and distractions had become the substance of his life. And other routines that frustrated him at first now comforted him, like the weekly visit by the gardeners who came to the neighborhood with their leaf blowers, the avid persistent roar of their machines outside his bedroom window. Recently he had been asked to paint a mural for a local school and had thought about using the gardeners as a motif. This morning had showered, dressed, and then packed his sketch pad, camera, and pencils into his bag. The years in California had temporarily abated the agonies of aging. He often wondered what life would have done to him had he stayed in London. If Alannah might now be visiting him in some care home or hospital, the distance in their ages a gulf they could no longer breach. His vitality gone, suffering her sympathy. He looked at the brushes lined up along the yellow shelf. He gathered them up, tied their black canvas pouch around them and placed them in the bag with the thought that he might work on a painting in the studio downtown later that day.

He opened his front door onto the patio and smiled at a young gardener bent over his leaf blower, the device strapped to his back. A scrawny boy in his late teens, with terra-cotta skin, he asked him where the leaves were taken once they had all been collected. The boy was reluctant to respond, as if fearing a confrontation, certain that this was the area his supervisor had told him to clear and that their work complied with the noise ordinances. He asked again, making clear this time there was no aggression, gesturing to the piles of leaves fallen from the Indian laurel. The supervisor, who had been friendly in the past, seeing the conversation in progress, walked over. He explained they had a permit for a disused patch of land they used as a burning ground on an undeveloped plot down toward Main Street. The plot had been sold a few years ago and although billboards had gone up advertising the new development, work had never started. He asked the supervisor if it would be OK for him to draw the men as they worked. He pointed inside to several unfinished canvases leaning against the wall. The supervisor smiled and shrugged, then turned to his men and told them in Spanish that this man was going to make them famous. They put down two cones at each end of the street, then set about pruning the highest branches of a plane tree that cast deep shade onto his neighbor's two-story concrete and glass house. As the branches fell to the ground light was let in onto the street. After the fallen branches had been collected in a tarpaulin and lifted onto the back of a pickup, the men set to work sweeping away the other fallen debris. Soon it was as if they had never been there.

After asking permission from the supervisor, he drove with the gardeners to the patch of disused ground where they disposed of the garden waste. They seemed wary at first as if he had been sent from the Department of Sanitation to report on them. He talked with the supervisor about the mural as he set the fire, dousing a stack of branches with gasoline. He stood back as the men tossed cuttings from the plane tree into the flames, emptying out the plastic sacks that held the leaves. The gardeners laughing with one another, salsa music coming from the little radio perched on the edge of their pickup. He wanted to take some photographs from behind the flames that he might use later as he prepared the mural. He walked to the back of the fire and reached into his bag for his camera. The canvas pouch that held the brushes had come undone and his fingers touched against their glossy bodies. As he looked into the rising smoke the hours in London with Alannah came back to him with a force they had not before: the rain on the skylight, the wilting lemon tree she would tease him for neglecting to water, the ring of fine creases where the pale skin folded at her neck. As he remembered he found himself running his fingers over the brushes as one might reach for the hand of a lover when woken in the night.

One by one, he tossed the brushes onto the fire: the filbert, the bright, the long-pointed. He had sat with Alannah in his studio in London teaching her their names three days before his sixty-fifth birthday. He did not think of that last night around her table in Tufnell Park, or the drive back with Delaney. How he sat alone and wept in his darkened studio, the salt tears hot on his face. Or how he had hammered at the table so hard that it splintered and left a gash across the palm of his hand. How he had been unable to hold a brush properly for a week afterward. Their nickeled brass brackets began to warp, the flames licking the ivory-black canvas of their pouch to vermilion, Prussian blue, yellow ochre, flake white. He watched the smoke rise in the sunlight of that California morning.

## '98 Mercury Sable

It's really the plainest of cars. Instantly forgettable. It's kind of like a Ford Mondeo but with a narrower, meaner, more pinched front. Slightly tinnier too. Less substantial. To be honest, I don't really know the first thing about cars. When we're out here in the States it's all I can do to make sure I don't turn left onto a rotary. There's nothing flashy or fancy about the Mercury Sable: it's dependable, boring, beloved of car-hire rental outlets, it's that kind of machine. I was happy to take it. It was cheap for one, by which I mean inexpensive, not badly made. We felt it was safe enough for the twins in the back. The guys at Midway even threw in a couple of child seats gratis, which I thought was good of them. I reasoned that even if I did bump it (last time out I'd clipped a mail van driving into Palm Springs, which, our lawyer later informed us, is a federal offense, and that wouldn't have looked good on my o-1 visa application), then it wouldn't be too expensive to repair. I'm not a natural driver, you see.

I was almost thirty before I passed my test. And only then after a weeklong intensive course in Southport back in England. I think they chose Southport as their base of operations as it's so mind-numbingly dull in the evening all you really want to do is stay in and read your highway code. After a day at the center I would come home to the moth-eaten, musty guest house on a terraced street and call Sophia from the pay phone in the hallway (my network had zero reception). She was pregnant with the twins at the time and I was always desperate for news. We'd agreed I had to be "road worthy" by the time they arrived. After all my coins had been gobbled up and I'd said a rushed good-night to Sophia, I would take a walk around the town and try to think of ways to pass the time. A northern seaside town in midwinter. It's about as grim as it gets. The last time I'd been there was on a school trip, so it felt like a particular kind of purgatory for me, as if my adult life had never happened. I mean, it's a compelling image: those tatty rows of shops, the strings of fairy lights, the angry sea. It's just not very practical.

After the first few nights, I gave up and stayed in my room, going over my highway code. Sitting there on flimsy reproduction furniture miming three-point turns and emergency stops. Pathetic really. The morning of the test was a nightmare. I don't think I'd ever been so nervous. If I'd had my way I would have stayed a card-carrying pedestrian, but the more we came out here to Los Angeles the more odd it seemed that I didn't drive. I'd tell people we met at dinner parties, decent, artistic, liberal people, that I was a nondriver and they'd look at me like I'd just told them I was illiterate. Not to mention the looks of perplexed machismo on the faces of valets when they saw me alighting from the passenger side. They looked at me as if I were an irredeemable drunk or mentally deficient. I'd taken to saying, loudly, "Do you fancy driving back, darling?" as we left restaurants. Sophia didn't find this funny at all.

The day of the test I was woken at 6 a.m. by Sophia's father telling me it was all about "the sports moment." Stepping up. Controlling my fear, not letting the fear control me. Sophia must have given him the number of the pay phone. I imagined him taking the corners of some tree-lined Hampshire B road in his Jaguar as he talked into his "hands free" on his way into the office. "There's a lot riding on this, Sebastian. Don't let us down." *Christ*, I thought. Nerves had always been a problem.

A week after my A Levels, I'd failed my test for the first time for speeding. I'd got it into my head that the bearded, bearlike examiner looked like a pedophile, which had really thrown me. It's amazing what stress can do. The next time was a decade later in Norwich, where Sophia was directing a play. The examiner, a friendly tall man with protruding front teeth and a luminous safety jacket, had just finished a cigarette when we got into the car. *You lucky bastard*, I thought. I'd given up a week earlier, which, in retrospect, was too much to take on, what with the driving as well. He'd been chatty through the test but toward the end—after it was clear to him that I'd failed (speeding, again)—I'll never forget how his mildly jaundiced face was completely unable to square the articulate man next to him with the inept driver in control of the shuddering, stammering car. In my defense, he'd thrown me from the outset, telling me that I had a strange accent and asking where it was from. Liverpool, I said, via Cambridge and, more recently, New York. Sophia had been directing off Broadway and we had been living out there for the past year. A gap in her schedule had brought her home for the summer. The final examination failure was in London a fortnight later, the day before we flew back to New York. It was an easygoing Rastafarian this time, with a gap-toothed smile, who laughed when I touched the curb during my reverse park. "Y'all be fine de next time, Mr. Carter, almost der, almost der," he chuckled. I went and got very drunk by myself in a bar just off the Portobello Road full of Polish builders on their lunch break.

So as you can imagine, that morning in Southport I was pretty nervous. Give me a script to edit, give me words to play with and my confidence knows no bounds but make me do something practical and in public and I am a wreck. I thought back to the last time I'd been crippled by nerves: my French oral examination at Sixth Form. The head of modern languages, Mr. Armstrong, had sensed my anxiety and suggested I take the edge off by having "a taste" before I went in. "A taste?" I said as we sat alone after class in the Portakabin that was the temporary classroom that term. "Yes, a taste," he said, "have a drink, lad."

The same strategy was deployed that morning in Southport. In the bottom of my wardrobe were six bottles of Premium Italian lager (the sourcing of which was a task in itself and had filled up at least one free evening) and a quarter bottle of vodka. I dressed, then downed a bottle of lager by my sink. Then another. Then for good measure took three long pulls on the tepid vodka. I then brushed my teeth vigorously and gargled with mouthwash. You can't be too careful. At the end of the test, when the lady examiner told me I had passed, all I could say was "Really? Are you *sure*?" On reflection, I suspect the driving school had some kind of arrangement with the examiner, who had seemed mildly distracted throughout the whole thing, at one point even composing a text message on her phone. But in

Southport I guess you have to take good reception where you can get it.

Anyway, all of this is by way of explaining that I am a cautious driver at the best of times and ever since the mail van incident, I could safely classify myself as extra cautious. Sophia was out here taking a bunch of meetings. Her *Hamlet* two summers at the Roundabout had been universally acknowledged as a triumph, noted for its "cinematic use of the stage." This had obviously made its way to the right people. So after working on a couple of independent films in New York that had gone down exceptionally well at the festivals, she'd been signed up by a studio. We'd been bouncing coast to coast for the past nine months and it was a time of great excitement in our lives. Excitement intensified by the imminent arrival of "No. 3," kicking, it seemed constantly, in that huge globe Sophia carried around her midriff.

We were driving out to Sophia's godmother's house for the weekend. The twins were in the back lobbying for a jack-in-the-box. We'd agreed on one "nonhealth meal" a week—Sophia's phrasing, not mine. Personally, I thought a bit of junk food did them no harm but Sophia was a little more militant. "Don't," she said, looking across at me, sipping from her bottle of Kombucha, a fermented Chinese tea.

As the twins' protests grew more fervent we agreed to stop at the next turnoff. The twins clearly needed to eat *something* and I could use a break as Sophia had proved completely inept at communicating the directions from the map on her iPhone, leading to several wrong turns along the way. Traditionally this had been my job and I now regretted making such a big deal of it, as it was clear Sophia was taking her revenge.

As we walked into the service station, a baby on each arm, my eye was drawn to a parked car in a row of empty spaces opposite ours. It was identical to the one we were driving, which wasn't that unusual, as ours—in design at least—looked pretty much like every other car on the freeway. However, what caught my eye was that this one, like ours, was a specific kind of electric blue. We'd picked ours out from among its dull cousins one hot morning on the Midway forecourt early on in our trip. It was mutually agreed to be our one concession to style. I had never seen one exactly like it here. In the back was a girl, about six, weeping, apparently inconsolable. *See what happens when you don't get them jack-in-the-box*, I thought and almost said as much to Sophia but decided to keep my powder dry. I imagined the argument the poor girl's parents were having inside. *Christ*, I thought, *just bite the bullet and get her the burger.*

We came out of the service station, loaded with dried fruit, Brazil nuts, goji berries, coconut water, and two strangely happy children somehow placated by Sophia's organic offerings. As I was opening the trunk, I saw the girl's father in the Mercury Sable across from ours smacking her, hard, across the front of her legs. The crack rang out across the lot. I reasoned that her mother was probably inside buying her that jack-in-the-box and it would all be OK when she came out. I didn't want Sophia to see as I was sure she'd cause a scene and I'd have to end up duking it out with some perfectly reasonable and responsible but deeply aggravated parent in the parking lot of a service station. Sophia is militantly anti-corporal punishment. She threatened to leave me six weeks into her pregnancy when I told her I could under-stand the arguments for it, calling me a "fucking Neanderthal" in the middle of the beer garden where we were having lunch with her parents. I looked away from the scene inside the car and down to its number plate, which began: S75. *Ha!* I thought, *like me: Sebastian, 1975.* I took it as a good omen.

An hour later I looked up briefly from the road and saw a flashing traffic sign with three lines of text; the middle line read "98 Mercury Sable." *Is that a freeway?* I thought. *Christ, is that the turn I was meant to take?* Sophia was asleep in the back with the twins. I had a premonition of her waking and suddenly shouting, "Mercury Sable, Sebastian, that was our bloody turn!" I looked down at the iPhone on my lap, clumsily thumbing at the map application. It told me we had another thirty miles before our first junction. *Phew*, I thought. *Close call.*

The traffic was moving nicely down the 101. I was beginning to loosen up, almost enjoying the drive. I was thinking about arriving at the lake house that evening. Wondering if Ernie, Sophia's godfather, would be around to take the boat out before supper. I unspooled my little fishing fantasy, imagining myself strolling triumphantly into the house, holding a giant trout aloft, presenting it to Sophia's godmother like a sacred chalice to a medieval queen. Ernie standing behind me, finally approving of something I did. I looked up again and there was the sign I had seen earlier, the words "98 Mercury Sable" in bright orange lights. I caught the bottom line this time too, "Lic: S75 FTT." *Sebastian, you idiot*, I thought, *Mercury Sable, it's not a road. It's a make of a car. It's the make of the car you're driving.* I heard Sophia's father's voice in my head: "It's a Sable, Sebastian, come on, focus."

A few minutes later and a little farther down the freeway I noticed the sign again. "98 Mercury Sable, Lic: S75 FTT." *Funny*, I thought, *that car in the service station was S75 and a Sable too.* Then it dawned on me: rampant commercialization. We had passed a series of sponsored motorways earlier, the Shirley Chen Junction, the Consuelo Latimer Bypass, and now they were even advertising used cars for sale on the freeway! Trying to sell you a used car during your commute. *God bless America*, I thought and floored the gas.

The sun was setting as we approached our turn-off to the lake house. A powder purple suffused across the skyline. Beautiful. I looked in the mirror at Sophia and the twins asleep in the back. There I was, king of the road. Well, a princeling at least. I imagined Ernie opening a beer for me and then I would take a long hot shower before dinner, listening to the crickets and cicadas starting up outside. I saw our junction and indicated to turn. Then I saw the sign again. Took it in. Fully this time. Each little orange light burning: "Child Abduction. 98 Mercury Sable. Lic: S75 FTT."

# Magda's a Dancer

"She's an *intellectual* actor. She brought a lot of thought to Ophelia when we workshopped *Hamlet* together at Columbia."

"What's she done? That space movie, right?"

"I didn't see it."

"It was terrible. Naturally. I saw her at Shakespeare in the Park a few years ago. She was completely insipid."

"Magda is just annoyed—can I tell them, baby?—Magda is just annoyed because a casting director I once worked with told me my darling wife looked like her. I took it as a compliment."

"It's not a compliment, Zachary. I was mortified."

"OK, OK. But, I gotta say this: at her best she kinda reminds me of a young Ingrid Bergman."

"Oh, come off it, Zack! That's like comparing Charlotte Church to Maria Callas."

"Charlotte who?"

"She's a young English soprano. Sang for Clinton once."

"She's Welsh, Harry."

"A young Welsh soprano."

"Glad to see I'm not the only fella who got a little sun this weekend, Harry."

"I was being very English about my sunbathing."

"He was being very silly. We were at Malibu Colony. He sat there all afternoon without any sunblock."

"Now I wake up every morning with pieces of my face falling off."

"It's like sleeping next to a leper."

"So you guys are subletting, right?"

"Just for the month."

"It's a great place. So much space. I always wondered who lived downtown."

"Itinerant Brits."

"It's funny, I was saying to Magda on the way up—by the way we parked in one of those vacant lots—the car is safe there, right?"

"It's fine."

"I was saying to her that when I was filming here last year I was actually given an escort to walk two blocks down to use the restroom."

"NO!"

"I was wearing stilettos at the time."

"I don't imagine downtown takes too kindly to drag artistes."

"Harry loves it down here, don't you? Says it's the only place he can get anything done."

"It's the only place in this whole city that actually feels like a city."

"Tell them what happened last night."

"I'd rather not. Are these lentils?"

"Harry!"

"I was waiting for Julia outside the parking lot down there."

"Come on. Tell the story properly."

"When you stand still for long enough out there you start to sink into this underworld that ordinarily you would have walked right through."

"Never stand still. First thing they teach you at Langley."

"It was incredibly quiet. No traffic. After about ten minutes I notice these guys are walking around and around the block, circling me. These three feral-looking guys."

"Tell them about the chair."

"Oh yeah, then this kid in a do-rag walks past carrying a chair. Puts it down directly opposite me, just under the scaffolding down there, outside Wigs and Slippers. It felt like he was marking me out or something. The whole thing was loaded with portent."

"Harry was terrified. Took him an hour to wind down."

"I wasn't terrified. It just felt completely lawless.
Like anything could happen. It was like being
back in the wild. It was exciting, I suppose,
in a way."

"Can you imagine him? Standing down there in his
espadrilles?"

"Hey buddy, it beats stilettos."

"Oh and you'll love this, Zack. He has this one
hoodie. He thinks it helps him blend in. But those
two sweet old queens we walked past the other
night, what did they say?"

"Nice top, babe. Is it designer?"

"He thinks it makes him look like one of those
cops from *The Wire*."

"It does make me look like one of the cops in
*The Wire*."

"Tell Harry how you two met."

"We were in middle school together."

"I've been kissing the same man for sixteen years."

"That's a lot of saliva."

"Harry!"

"Sorry. Go on. I'm interested."

"Magda's mom ran the drama center at school."

"I watched him auditioning for a play, doing this series of little comedy skits he'd written, in front of the whole year. I thought—*there is a brave man*."

"Not a handsome or a witty man, just a brave man you notice."

"So my mom cast us both in a production of *Tartuffe*."

"Which translation?"

"The Wilbur, you read it?"

"No, but I know his poetry."

"So in a sweeping feat of nepotism Mom casts us both . . ."

"Sorry, Magda, I interrupted you there."

"It's OK, Harry."

"Yeah, sorry, honey. Carry on."

"... in this school production of *Tartuffe*."

"Magda was a genius, Harry. I mean she'd been coached by Wanda, her mom, since she was a little girl."

"Oh, stop it."

"I'm serious, honey. And let me tell you both this, hand on heart, Magda has more talent in her little finger than the actress we were discussing earlier whose name I won't mention."

"Zachary, you're embarrassing me."

"What do you do now, Magda?"

"You're a landscaper, aren't you?"

"Studying to be. I just signed up for a three-year MSc."

"But Magda trained in ballet initially, at the Joffrey. My girl's a dancer."

"The ballet was my first love."

"She used to come home with these bruised knees."

"So why the change of career?"

"Couldn't make it work. Plus USC has offered
me a scholarship."

"That's wonderful! Congratulations. We should
toast it. Julia?"

'To Magda!'

"To Magda, but here's the kicker: the scholarship
was \$50,000; the fees are, wait for it, \$58,000."

"You're kidding?"

"I should also add, in my wife's defense, she's
actually training to be a landscape gardener NOT a
landscaper: the former dealing with urban planning
and environmental issues and so forth, the latter
blowing leaves off your lawn."

"Maybe the four of us should all go into business.
A team of artists turned landscape gardeners.
We could buy a pickup."

"Harry, let him finish."

"Sorry."

"So, OK, where was I? So we looked at our finances
and figured we'd be better off taking the debt and
moving out here. Didn't we, honey?"

"Do you miss New York?"

"Me? Oh sure. Terribly. But Zachary needs to be out here. Tell them about the pilot, Zachary."

"Oh, a series I was attached to just got green-lit after the pilot. It's a recurring role."

"Oh, well done, Zack!"

"Thanks, honey. It's a pain in the ass though. The network aren't going to use me until the second episode. Who watches the second episode? And I'm going to miss all that camaraderie of the first day on set."

"Maybe you should just turn up. Announce yourself: Hi. I'm Zack. I'm not on until episode two but I just wanted to touch base."

"Harry."

"What?"

"He's got a point. What about you, sweetheart? How are things looking?"

"Why do you think I'm here? No one is making movies in London. The industry is on its knees. I mean even when it was going full pelt, at its height, we were still only making five or six a year. There are massive financial constraints now. Financiers are less willing to invest in anything, no matter how commercial the idea is. And of course, on top of that much less, if any, commitment to serious cinema. Government subsidies have dried up. This recession back home looks like it's going to be a double-dip . . ."

"Would anyone like to go for coffee after the lecture?"

"Notice the silence of our guests, Harry? That wasn't funny."

"Sorry."

"Anyway. Not great is the answer. But we got sidetracked. Where were we?"

"*Tartuffe.*"

"So it's been a roller coaster from there. On and off. Off and on. But we're still riding it, aren't we, baby?"

"All the way."

"How old were you when you got married?"

"Twenty-four."

"That's young."

"Yeah well we'd been kinda shilly-shallying back and forth for years. After a year apart—where I badly sowed my wild oats across the lesser repertory theaters of the Eastern seaboard— we'd hooked up again, we were both living in Brooklyn just a few streets apart at the time. Famously, this is the period of our life when Magda looked me straight in the eye one night after making love and told me she could never love me like I loved her."

"Ouch."

"I know. Julia would never say that to you, right?"

"She would probably say 'I could never love you like I love myself.'"

"Harry!"

"Sorry, darling, I was kidding."

"I want a fag."

"Baby, we've quit."

"Oh bugger off."

"So, wait, back to the story: she tells you
that and . . ."

"And I say, 'OK. OK.' Maybe I'll call you sometime.
I go away, take a job in Boston—playing a workman
in *Vanya* at the Shubert—for a couple of months.
And I do a lot of growing up. So when I get back
to town I give her a call."

"I hadn't heard from him but he was still kind
of on my radar. And you know what, when the
phone rang, I'd just that minute hung up from a
conversation with a girlfriend who'd been asking
about him. It was eerie."

"So I call her. And we talk. And it's nice. So nice.
I say look, it just doesn't feel as good with anybody
else. Simple as that."

"Wow."

"However . . ."

"You'll notice, Harry, that there's always a *however*
with Zack."

"*However*, there's the small matter of the girl I'm
dating at the time. Complicated by the fact
she is also my co-lead in a new two-hander I'm

doing at the Schoenfeld. You know it, Julia, it used to be the Plymouth."

"I went along to watch one night. Afterwards when we were sitting together in the empty theater, I said, 'Zachary, you have to get rid of her.'"

"What, like, bump her off?"

"I wish, Harry. It was harder than that."

"We're out of wine. I'm going to go to 7-Eleven. Harry, do you want to come with?"

"Why don't we all go? We can't really leave our guests here alone."

"Hey, I'm game. We stand more chance of survival if we move in a pack."

"Yes, let's all go. Fun!"

"Keys. You got the keys, Harry?"

"Check."

"Did you see that guy's face in the elevator! Priceless. He sounded just like my grandpa."

"And that woman he was with! She looked pissed. Bad date. How old do you think he was?"

"Sixty-four? Sixty-five?"

"He looked like he knew what he was doing."

"You think, Zack? He reminded me of that extra from our show, after we transferred. What was his name?"

"I know who you mean. Same smile. But hey, at least he'd got her up to his apartment."

"But they were going down."

"He's probably still getting over the divorce. These things take time."

"Zachary, that's cruel. Julia! Where did you get that?"

"A bloke in the 7-Eleven."

"Good work! Need a light?"

"I'll use the car lighter. Zack, finish your story."

"Where was I?"

"You were about to murder an actress."

"Thanks, Harry. Shall we open one of these?"

"I'll do it. Carry on with the story."

"Ain't much to say. I rode out a couple of difficult weeks at the theater. All our friends were like, 'so when are you guys getting married then?' And I look at her, and I'm like, so shall we?"

"And I tell him that I don't see why not."

"And that was that. Nuptial bliss ever since."

"And now the big move West."

"I know, exciting times for Zachary and Magda. Right, honey?"

"You said it."

"So, Zack, are you moved in yet to the new place?"

"No, sweetheart, we've been staying with friends in Eagle Rock. The move proper is next weekend."

"My mom is driving Zachary's old car across from Minneapolis."

"No!"

"Yes. This'll be Wanda's first time in LA. Ever."

"Eighty hours cross-country with only her Isley Brothers cassettes for company."

"That's incredible. Has the music stopped? Put something on, Harry."

"I'm drunk."

"Hey Harry, you got any M. J. on that thing?"

"Sure."

"You got *Thriller?*"

"Yeah, we've got *Thriller.*"

"OH, MY GOD! THAT IS HILARIOUS!"

"Where did you guys learn to do that?"

"Middle school. Her zombie moves are unreal, right?"

"That's brilliant. You ever hit hard times you can take that on tour."

"A *Thriller* Re-Enactment Troupe."

"You know it, sister. Hey, where's your restroom? I mean your *toy-let.*"

"It's on the left."

"Is she OK?"

"I think she's just stretching, Harry."

"Maria Callas does that to people."

"Turn it up a bit. Look . . ."

"Christ, is she, is she doing . . . ballet?"

"Shhhhh! Watch . . ."

"She's really, really . . ."

"Good."

"It's beautiful. Completely . . . beautiful."

"What I miss? Ah, Magda's doin' the ballet."

"Zack! She's incredible."

"I'm completely mesmerized."

"Harry, give me a hand moving this—what do you call this?"

"A banquette."

"A bonk-ette. Love it. Help me move it.
She needs more space."

"She's incredible."

"Harry, turn it up.
OK, Magda, honey, do it again, from the top."

# Acknowledgments

Thanks are due to Sarah Chalfant and Alba Ziegler-Bailey at the Wylie Agency for their continued support. And to Alexandra Pringle at Bloomsbury and Jill Bialosky at W. W. Norton & Company for guiding this book to life. Thanks also to Alice Eve, Heather and Neal Callow, Tom Bannister and Eva Chen for showing me various aspects of California in their time. To early readers and improvers Andrew Motion, Will Goodlad, and Edmund Gordon. And to American friends David Shook and Zinzi Clemmons for casting their scrupulous eyes over these stories. Special thanks are due to William Boyd, who suggested it might be an idea to write a whole book of stories about Los Angeles.

## Note on the Author

**ADAM O'RIORDAN** was born in Manchester in 1982 and read English at Oxford University. In 2008 O'Riordan became the youngest Writer in Residence at The Wordsworth Trust, the center for British Romanticism. His first collection of poetry, *In the Flesh*, won a Somerset Maugham Award in 2011. He is academic director of the Writing School at Manchester Metropolitan University. *The Burning Ground* is his first collection of short stories.

adamoriordan.com
@oriordanadam

## A Note on the Type

The text of this book is set in Bembo, which was first used in 1495 by the Venetian printer Aldus Manutius for Cardinal Bembo's *De Aetna*. The original types were cut for Manutius by Francesco Griffo. Bembo was one of the types used by Claude Garamond (1480–1561) as a model for his Romain de l'Université, and so it was a forerunner of what became the standard European type for the following two centuries. Its modern form follows the original types and was designed for Monotype in 1929.